Hell's Earth

Inspirational
Demon

PUBLISHED BY:
    PETE TROLENE
    PHILADELPHIA, PA

DISTRIBUTED BY:
    KINDLE - E BOOK
    CREATE SPACE
    WWW.CREATESPACE.COM
    WWW.AMAZON.COM

ISBN# 9780615961040Txu 1-778-148
    Hells Earth
    Copyrighted 2011
    pete john trolene
    ALL RIGHTS RESERVED
    petetrolene@yahoo.com
    COVER ART/DESIGNS

The story begins
when one of the Devil's
Generals tries to escape from
Hell.
Jon is introduced as an alcoholic/addict
who is trying to forget a family tragedy.
He is joined buy a boy who carries
something powerful.
A Holy War in unholy Hell erupts.
The Cherubs are called to
fight for "Heaven's Gates"
The lands impervious to Hells
nature are called
Hell's Earth

COMING SOON

END of 2015

WE WILL BE

GODS

"A must read for
the spirit in us all"

I, Anonamously...

Dedicated to my family and friends of
past and present.
To all those who lost their lives
or the lives of a loved one to the
Devil's advocate "addiction".

Special thanks to Suchi and Larry Jordan
for their inspiration and spiritual wisdom.

Thank you to all the angels and guardians
who protect us from the forces of evil.

"Threre are two things
on this world
that are two-dimentional
that we can see with
our eyes;
our reflections
and
our shadows"

PJT 3

"NICE DEMON"

The demon was hiding up against a wall in the building. Through the window he could see the other demon soldiers pass by in the street. They were looking for him and his precious cargo. He had been hiding in the shadows of the abandon buildings for days. The shadows hid him well. After a while he would move to another building. There he would sit and wait quietly.

All of Hell's creatures were looking for him, not just the soldiers. Hell's bounty hunters, trackers and demon cults like the "Saist" also gave chase to the hunt. The "General" was out numbered. He was trying to make it to the outskirts of the city. Once he reached the city limits the land was open and he would be able to make a run for Hell's Earth. Only there will he and his precious cargo will be safe. If they catch him before he reaches Hell's Earth then he will surely die and all we know will be in great danger.

The skyscrapers stood in the flames while everything around them crumbled. Burning building by burning building the General crossed through the heart of the city.

Finally, he reached the end of the city. He could now make a straight run for Hell's Earth. There was so much for him to gain and everything to lose. He must reach the Holy Lands of Hell.

The skies were red. The clouds were outlined in flames. The sun had a burnt orange center with a charred-black ring around it. The land that lied ahead of him was of bare red sand that blew around in the heated wind. Bolts of lightning exploded in the distance as the temperature gave the horizon a hazy look. This land is not just any wasteland. This land is Hell!

1

The sun that never sets was turning into its dusk. It was time for the general to make a run for it.

As the General of the Devil he was given many powers, fortunes, and talents here in Hell. One who is bound here for eternity would not usually give up such power. He must have had a powerful epiphany of some sort. One that was close to his heart perhaps. A seed must have been planted. It bloomed all through his veins and strong enough for him to gain a moment for him to catch his sanity. He had the opportunity to escape and he had enough hope to believe it was possible to leave this Hell, his Hell.

He waited for the best moment to run. He had not seen any demons for a while. So, he took a deep breath and started to run. He was running as fast as he could. He crossed over the final street and into the open. He did not even bother to look back because he knew that they already spotted him. He had trained them well. And they did spot him. The chase began.

The general was faster than any animal on earth and one of the fastest beings in Hell. He knew the wasteland well. This hell has been his home for several centuries.

The general was way ahead of the demon soldiers and their trackers. He could not hide anymore if he tried. They could notice him changing. There was no turning back. He was once one of the damned, a slave to the Devil. Ordered to serve him when called upon and then left to walk the red fiery wasteland once the dirty deeds were done. Now, he is the Devil's most wanted.

His appearance had changed. His tail and horns had fallen off, yet his eyes remained blood red like the other damned creatures. The General had grown hair like a lion's mane. Its color had changed from pitch black to the shiniest of silver. His body had become bright red and became brighter as he thruster forward. The General looked up and saw bright white light. There in his sights was Hell's Earth.

The General carried a satchel. He held it tightly. The Damned Soldiers were not only after the General but they also wanted what was in the bag. What was in the bag was a book. It was a personal book of the Devil.

The General ran faster and faster, cutting through the desert sand. He ran faster than he ever ran before. His running had become so strong he started to lift off the ground in between steps covering more and more ground with every leap.

There was a lot of power and energy in the General's running and leaping. The General's red-hot body had become so hot that it turned into a solid metal rendering his body motionless as he soared through the air. Everything fell silent. The General thought it was the end for him until the miracle happened. A bright light powered its way out from the inside of the General. The light seeped through the cracks of the metal until its shell had exploded off.

The General had finally transformed. His body had evolved into a glittery-white skinned angel. A golden glow radiated off his body and for the first time in a long time, the General shrugged a smile. He had shed his skin of the damned that he has worn for so long and now wore the skin of God's angels. Only his eyes still remained red. He was not yet all the way free from the bondage of the Devil.

The General continued running without losing a step.
He was almost there. Once he had reached the land in the light he would be out of harm's way and redemption would be his.

He knew how to use the book. He knew how to open a stairway to heaven. Once he reached Hell's Earth and fully transformed into an angel he would be able to work the powers of the book and go to heaven.

A sandstorm had erupted from the east. It was moving towards the General's direction. The General redirected his run towards the west.

Another sandstorm erupted in the west. There was only one way to go now, straight ahead. The two storms raced towards the center of the Generals direction. The storms were trying to cut the General off from making it to Hell's Earth. It was a race to the finish.

The General was almost there. Only 30 yards to go and he was running at top speed.

Suddenly, a volcano of sand erupted right in between the General and Hell's Earth. The sandstorm had beaten him to the front. Rising 50ft. above the General, the tall mountain of red sand formed into a fiery red dragon.

This did nothing to slow down the General. He did not come this far to give up now. His faith and desperate heart led him to charge towards the belly of the beast. The General lunged at the dragon. The dragon, however, lowered its head, opened its mouth and plunged its tongue into the General's chest. The General let out a gasp as he was stopped abruptly. Silence fell amongst the ears of the General.

The dragon transformed into a giant demon with the dragons tongue turning into the demon's arm. The demon's hand clenched the General's heart.

The General looked into the demon's eyes. He now recognizes the demon creature. It is the Devil himself. After all, it was his book. It was one of only a few sacred books that held the secret's of the universe. The Devil

16

has plans for this book. The Devil wants his book.

"There is no escape and you will go through a century of pain for dishonoring me!" said the Devil in a deep dark language. Then the Devil squeezed his and snapped the General's heart. Blood ran down the Devil's hand and stained the General's white-glittery skin. The General's head rolled to the back of his neck. His eyes were solid black. He looked empty but he mumbled something.

"In the name of our father!" said the General. The General used all his might to take the satchel from his side and throw it towards the lighted land of Hell's Earth.

The Devil turned to try and catch the book. As he turned he ripped the heart out of the General. The Devil roared as the book soared passed him. He was too late. The book had crossed over into the light and vanished. The Devil burned his hand as he tried to go after the book. The book was now safe from him for the moment.

The Devil turned back around towards the General. He saw that his demon traitor, his General, had turned into golden-white sand and blew away with the wind. This had meant that the General had fulfilled his reconciliation and he was now at peace.

The Devil looked at his army with great disappointment. The soldiers were now filled with fear. The General had escaped and the book was protected within the realm of Hell's Earth. They knew they were going to be held accountable. They knew they were all going to pay.

Jon Welsh had just got out of rehab a few months ago. He's been battling alcohol and drug addiction ever since his wife, Olivia, had taken her own life.

While Olivia was pregnant, her hormones caused her to fall into major depression. She had a psychotic break down and hung herself. She took her own life and her unborn baby's life with just 2 weeks left till birth.

Jon used to think he had it all. He was just starting out in life. He was a young promising officer in the military and was advancing very quickly. He advanced in rank because of his outstanding service and performance in combat. He had been a leader ever since he first joined the service.

After their death, Jon became depressed himself. A military doctor had prescribed him some narcotics for his depression. But Jon could not shake it. He could not get the image out of his head. He would take more of the medication then needed, thinking it would stop the image. It did not work. He easily became hooked on the prescription medications. When the pills no longer worked he started drinking. He would drink until he blacked out. His heavy drinking eventually led to his discharge from the military.

After his discharge Jon spent all of his time roaming the streets. He was looking for a fix. Any fix. He was looking for any way to numb out his pain.

Today was different. He is clean today. He hasn't had a drink or a drug in 5 days. He relapsed after one day of leaving the rehab and has been getting high ever since. He's been sleeping at the homeless shelter and they won't allow anyone that is intoxicated to stay there. By the grace of God, today Jon has a choice.

Every day, Jon walks past the last place he saw his wife alive. It was at their home along the city's border. He had lost the house long ago to for closure. But he still walks and

stands outside of the house. He often
wonders if their spirit may still be around.
He prays to her, hoping she can hear him.
He is hoping she forgives him for whatever
he had done to push her to the limit. He
blames himself for what happened with her.
He often blames himself for things beyond
his control.

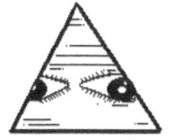

3

Dylan is 12 years old. He has the intelligence of an adult and the wisdom of a noble knight. He receives good grades in school and is interested in music and chemistry. He wasn't the most popular kid. He only had a handful of friends. It wasn't his style to be the center of attention. Dylan did not like phony people and wanted his friendships to be true.

He had two best friends named Mark and Doug. They all were good kids and true friends.

Doug was always thinking of new adventures. He always had crazy ideas that pushed passed the limits. Mark and Dylan liked that best about him. They knew Doug would always be there for them even if it meant he had to get his hands dirty.

23

They were kids that loved adventure. They would explore wooded trails with their bikes and hike the trails nobody else dared to ride. They would have treasure hunts along the way. They would make maps of their adventure and expand their routes the next time they came back.

They always found some kind of an adventure, even if they went out on their own. They would share their stories with each other the next day and explore it again together when they had sleepovers.

Dylan sometimes would day dream of going to battle like they did in the middle-ages with swords and shields. He always rode a horse and had his two best friends with him. They would ride side-by-side all the way to the end.

They were true friends at heart and they all believed in honor.

4

  The school bell rang and the classes let out where Dylan attended school. The boys met up in the cafeteria. They gave each other a greeting and walked over to the lunch tables and sat down. Mark had a piece of paper rolled in his hand. He unrolled it and laid it on the table. It was a map that he had drawn during his class. It was a map of their neighborhood. It showed the areas that they had already explored and where they didn't explore.

"What about here?" Dylan asked as he pointed to a spot on the map.

"That's that old abandon building. I think that is connected to the old run-down church," stuttered Doug. "We can see it from the bike trails beyond the trees. Do you want to check that out tonight?" asked Doug.

"Sure, make a list of treasures that we might find tonight," replied Dylan. "We will see who can find the most stuff. Winner gets first pick of the pile."

"We're not supposed to go there," whimpered Mark. "There's a fence around it and I heard it was haunted."

"Don't be such a bitch!" said Doug.

All the boys laughed.

"I'm not scared. I'm just giving you a warning," said Mark. "Who knows what we'll find?"

"I'll bring some bolt cutters to cut a hole in the fence" said Doug.

"Great," replied Dylan. "We'll meet up at the fence after school and baseball practice. I'll catch up with you guys!" Dylan shook his head to reassure his friends that he will be there as he walked away.

Jon walked along the waterfront overlooking the city. The sun was starting to set beyond the city 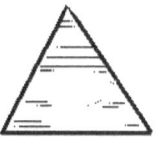 bridges. It was a really nice view of a city on Earth. But nothing in life seemed to give Jon any pleasure anymore. Jon sat down on a park bench until the sun had set completely. He still hadn't had a drink. The past five days he has been in a detoxification process from heroin, cocaine and alcohol. The shelter has a policy that all new residence must be on a 5 day black out. He was not aloud off the premises for five days. Today

27

is his first time out of the shelter and on his own. They gave him a chance on his honor.

He could feel the stress moving in on him. The cravings to get high crowded his brain. He didn't want to get high and he didn't want to go back to the homeless shelter. "At least it won't be so bad if I was all numbed out," said Jon to himself. "I might as well just go get high. Maybe it will be better this time. I just need a little to take the edge off."

Jon could not stay still and his hands were shaking.

"I can't make it stop!" said Jon out loud about his hands shaking and his thoughts racing. He could not handle it anymore.

Jon gave in to his cravings and he started to walk to the inner city for drugs. His mind was made up. His wheels were spinning and it was almost impossible for him to change his mind by this point. In a moment's time, he went from fighting his urges to giving in to his racing thoughts. He just wants it to stop.

The thoughts of her death raced through his head. Thoughts of world disasters, human destruction and gruesome horrors all ran through his mind. His mind flashed through the history of life destroying itself. Various events from his life played out in his mind in a blink of his eye. He was searching for an answer. He was looking for a different answer then the truth. He had his answer. It was an answer that he did not want to hear. They were dead. In truth, he wanted them back.

He wanted them back but what he needed was to stop hurting himself. He could not let the trauma pass and it haunted him. He kept hearing voices that would not stop chanting. They kept calling his name whenever his mind would get racing thoughts.

Jon would use alcohol and heroin to ease his pain, but the voices still kept coming. They were strongest whenever Jon used up his entire stash of heroin and he would start going into with drawl.

Once you are in, there is no getting out. Like most addicts, he needed his drugs to numb out. He needed the drugs to quiet the voices in his head.

The Devil grabbed a smaller demon that was standing nearby and through him into the light of Hell's Earth.

"Go get my book," yelled the Devil. The demon disintegrated immediately. The Devil gave out a roar and tried to calm himself with heavy breathing. He stood there thinking to himself. Not moving but breathing every so heavy. His breathing alone struck fear into his army. He took a look down the border of Hell's Earth and then again in the other direction. He looked all around Hell's Earth and saw that there was no way for him to go inside. He stared straight into the dome light of Hell's Earth. The Devil saw something. He could see where the book had landed. It was blurry but two images were absolutely clear. The Devil saw the old set of church doors with two A.A. symbols inside a circle. The next image was of a bearded, longhaired, ragged looking man. It was Jon.

The Devil laughed under his breath and then out loud, as he was pleased with what he saw. The Devil knows the weaknesses of mankind. The Devil knew how to get to Jon.

30

7

Jon kept hearing voices in his head. It was the same voices from the dreams he was having. The voices were very soft-spoken. Jon sometimes thought that the voices were actually angels singing to him. He thought they were trying to tell him something. Jon could never tell what they were trying to say. The  voices would overlap each other and the sound would become distorted in a rhythmic sort of way.

Jon had been walking through a wooded trail on his way into the city. The trail strangely led him to an old building. "That voice. It…" Jon started to say but then another softer voice cried out, "Go inside!"

Jon was startled. He quickly looked up to see a set of doors with an emblem painted on them. The emblem was of two letter A's and a triangle in a circle. A sign Jon has seen before.

"Hey man, are you coming to the meeting?" a voice interrupted the deep thought Jon was having. Jon was staring at the ivy that grew all around the old church door and onto the roof. Jon spotted an old man standing on the porch that was hidden from the ivy.

"It's an AA meeting but all addictions are welcome tonight," said the old man politely. "Is this your first time here? I never have seen you around here before?"

No response from Jon.

"Well, listen. My name is Bill. I've been coming here for 20 years. And I've managed to get 18 of them sober. Let me tell you something. There's something special about this old church. Do you want to really know why I come here?"

Just then an older lady stuck her head out of the doors and said to Bill,

"Hey, Bill the meeting is getting ready to start." "Alright, I'll be right in," replied Bill.

"Congratulations on your chip!" exclaimed the woman. "Thank you, Mary" replied Bill. Mary went back inside. Jon looked up at Joe and finally broke his silence.

"I thought you said you had 18 years?" asked Jon.

"I said I had 18 years sober, but not when I was sober. I am sort of just coming back," said Bill as he started to shake his head. "Anne, My wife died last year. Well, I couldn't…" Bill paused. Suddenly, the happy fellow broke down and sadness filled his eyes.

"…I'm not making any excuses, but I just couldn't take it anymore and I needed a break!" Bill said quickly and stubbornly as he wanted to change the subject.

"Well, I got to go. Nice meeting you," said Bill as he turned around.

"So, why do you come here?" asked Jon. He asked almost demandingly before Bill walked away. The old man turned around, smiled and said,

"You'll find your answer right there," Bill pointed his finger toward the set of doors. There were two emblems on the doors. Each door had the letter A. Together they formed a triangle.

Jon looked bewildered for a moment and then said,

"I am sorry for your loss. I know your pain. Believe me, when I tell you, I know your pain!"

Bill stopped and looked into Jon's eyes. He knew about that look in his eyes. He saw it every time he looked into a mirror.

"Such a young age to start carrying that kind of baggage," Bill mumbled to Jon.

"What's your name son?" Bill asked.

"Jon" he responded.

"Jon, the reason I come here is to get some answers. While I was searching for the answers I managed to get 18 years sober. I can't promise anything, Jon. I can't even tell you how you will get your answers. I can only tell you what worked for me. The answers to my questions were around these rooms of A.A. Most of the time I got my answers from other people, sometimes it was a phrase hanging on a wall or something someone said, or just the sound of one voice helping another. But sometimes…" Bill leaned over to whisper in Jon's ear,

34

"… It was the fresh coffee and pastries made by Ms. Mary that got me to keep coming back on many days." Bill chuckled as he started to walk away.

Bill paused and turned around.
He then said to Jon,
"You know they say he works through people. Let me ask you something Jon, when you pray to God, how do you expect to get an answer?" Bill paused for a moment.
Then Bill gave an answer for Jon,
"Everyone has a different answer and it comes in different ways. To each, their own, Jon! But you! You have to be the one to recognize when your answer comes. And then you, only you, take action!"

   Jon stood there silently as he watched Bill enter the A.A. doors.
   Every time Jon went to a meeting it was always for the wrong reasons. He only attended a meeting if the parole officers demanded it or if he needed to claim his whereabouts. He always would leave out the back doors just as the meeting started. Then, he would go to the liquor store and

chug a pint of vodka before returning to the meeting in time for the end.

Jon was smart but lately he has not been honorable. He was not thinking right. He has been using his intellect to swindle people. Jon would only do crime when he was drinking and getting stoned. That was mostly all the time. He would pull off little crimes to get money for his drug habit. The crimes Jon did were called "paper crimes". This type of crime was not violent or obscene. This gave Jon an excuse to minimize his wrong doings. But stealing is still a crime no matter how it is done.

Lately, Jon would do anything in order to get a fix. He would do anything to stay high. Jon hardly ever went to bed. He would drink until he passed out. And Jon never woke up, he just came through.

Only tonight, this night, Jon did not need a fix. This night he has a choice. Tonight still belongs to him.

8

Dylan was a very good kid. He had good grades in school and he had an excellent home environment.

Dylan's mother and father were good people. They were always working hard looking for cures for the sick. They both attended college  and met each other their junior year. Dylan's mother and father married and had Dylan shortly after. Three years after Dylan's birth they had Dylan's sister, Jessica.

After his parents had graduated college they had opened their own laboratory. They became connected with some political people who helped supply them with grants. The grants were used to support their research.

Dylan believed that his parents and the politicians were the people who really made a difference in the world. He often wondered if other people could see the good in his parents.

There was always good vibes coming from their family. They were all always a positive influence to each other and those around them. It was almost as if they were magically connected with each other.

Dylan learned things quickly. He was a little quicker than most kids his age. His father taught him everything he knew about the world at a young age. Dylan adopted his father's knowledge and charisma. His father's teachings came from the heart. Honesty, trust, loyalty and how good things happen to those who do good things are some of the teaching that his father bestow to his son.

"Treat others as how you would want to be treated!"

Dylan believed in his father and in his father's words. He believed his father was the wisest of all the wisest men.

Some of his teachings stemmed from the Bible, like the Ten Commandments. Other

teachings came from his father's own
experiences in life. Some of those lessons
Dylan did not understand. Dylan knew the
difference of right from wrong but did not
understand why some people actually
choose to do wrong. This made Dylan angry.
Dylan knew that there was much more to
be learned about the universe and about life.
He gave the thought, "a hundred years ago,
people thought they were the most advanced
beings in the universe. They thought that
they could not get any more advanced then
what they already were. Today,
some people say the same thing.
And yet we get more and more
advanced every day."
Dylan believed that there was more to his
life as well. He believed that there was
something special waiting. Something he
still had to learn. He felt it in his heart. He
had the faith that something more powerful
existed and he had the hope that his faith
was right.

Dylan finished school and went to baseball practice. His sister, Jessica, was practicing softball on the field next to his.

Dylan stepped up into the batter's box. He tapped to home plate with the tip of his bat and got set in his stance.

The pitch was fast, the crack of the bat was loud. Dylan hit the ball way back....

Ironically, Jessica stepped up to the plate on the other field at the same time as Dylan. She swung her bat and hit the ball, way back....

All of the players stood up. Everyone in the entire ballpark simultaneously held a breath. They all eagerly watched as the baseballs on each field soared in the air. Both of the balls were hit high in the air. It

41

seemed like forever for the balls to land. Finally, Dylan's ball landed over the fence for a homerun. A tremendous roar of applause filled the air, but only after another roar of applause came from the other baseball field. The entire ballpark was filled with excitement and cheer. Heads were turning back and forth as the parents and spectators were curious as to what had happened on the opposite fields. Was it possible to have two homeruns happen right next to each other at the same time?

Dylan rounded second base and saw another player rounding second base on the other field. He could not see who the player was.

Dylan did see a person running from the other field. He was not a player but a fan. He was yelling, "She got a homerun! She did it! She did it!"

"She?" thought Dylan to himself. He was curious as to what had happened on the other field. He wondered if it was his sister. He had a good feeling it was her.

Right before Dylan took the swing that gave him the homerun, a form of energy filled his body and was released with his swing. He could not help to think the same thing happened to his sister.

After baseball practice Dylan met up with his sister and they walked home.

"I heard you got a home run!" said Jessica to Dylan.

"Yes I did. I heard you got one too. How did you know that I got a homerun?" asked Jessica.

"Actually, I saw it. Well, I saw you rounding second base and figured the rest out from the crowd cheering." Dylan gave her a nod as if he was proud of her.

Dylan and Jessica arrived home to find that their mom and dad were not home yet. Dylan and Jessica went into the kitchen and got something to eat. They ate while they did their homework.

"I thought you were going to go out with your bozo friends?" asked Jessica.

"Yeah, I was going to but then I wouldn't get home until later and you would be here all by yourself. Besides, those two guys will be around all night. I'll catch up with them later. They don't mean any harm, there just…well, you know…"

43

"Morons!" said Dylan and Jessica at the same time as they laughed out loud.

"Jinx, you owe me a soda-pop!" They both said out loud at the same time.

"Jinx!" Again they repeated the same words at the same time. They laughed and laughed.

There was a lot of love between them. It always glowed whenever they were together.

10

Jon took a seat at the back of the meeting despite him really not wanting to be there. He just wanted to go on with his mission but he was short some money. Jon thought he might be able to hustle up some money here. He barely had enough for a bag of heroin and he needed some supplies to "fix up". He thought about taking the money out of the donation plate.

Jon thought to himself, "I don't need all the money. I'll just take a few bucks for what I need. Besides, all of the donations that I gave before, they owe me!"

Jon was not thinking straight. Jon has not thought right since the tragedy. His condition was getting worse. His mind could not think of anything else except for the death of his family or the cravings to get high.

45

Jon did not recognize anyone. That was good; he thought nobody could identify him. He did not want to talk to anyone. He didn't want to be mean but Jon thought he had no more happiness in him. Therefore, he had nothing good to share.

The meeting was about to start and everyone took a seat. There were two men that sat behind a folding table in front of the room. One man was to conduct the meeting. The other person was a guest spokesman. About ten people were attending tonight's meeting.

"Is this anyone's first meeting?" the man with the mustache asked out loud. Jon tilted his hat down to cover his eyes and sat quietly. He didn't say a word. Nobody said anything. The room was silent. Jon could hear his heart beating at a rapid pace. He was beginning to sweat underneath his hat's brim.

"Could somebody please read the hand out, out loud?" ask the man chairing the meeting.

Some of the other guests began to read some of the papers they handed out. They always did this at the beginning of most meetings. Jon heard the words before. Tonight, they echoed inside his head.

Jon could not stay still. He kept swaying back and forth in his seat. He was fidgety and nervous. It began to bother him that he did not know anyone. Paranoia started closing in on Jon. He was in a room with ten people and he felt alone. He had not felt like this since he was a kid. Panicking, Jon looked at each person in the room and started to imagine what they were thinking. He could hear their voices rambling in his head.

He imagined he heard the pretty woman thinking about the troubles with her teenage daughter. He imagined he heard the old man wondering if he took his medication today. He heard the young Italian fellow in the corner wondering if he is the best looking guy in the room. The businessman was thinking,
"I need a drink!"
The chunky middle-aged man was thinking, "I cannot believe my mother is making me go to this stupid thing!" The room was beginning to spin.

Jon saw a handsome looking fellow sitting to his far left side. He heard the man's thoughts of

"I'd do her!" The man's thoughts were about the girl sitting next to him. Jon glanced at the woman. She looked like Jon's wife.

Jon quickly stood up. When he did, he caught a glimpse of a gruesome looking person wearing goggles who was across the meeting room and in the back rooms. Jon's head suddenly came into focus. Jon's eyes stared to see the person again. He could not see. Jon sat back in his chair to take another look but someone had moved in front of Jon and blocked his view. When Jon was able to look again, the person was gone.

The chairperson finished with the readings and it was now time for the speaker. The speaker was an older guy with medium long hair and a gray beard. He wore sunglasses, even though they were inside, and a denim jacket. When he spoke it was in a calm, deep voice. He spoke with a Boston accent and he had the appearance of a hardcore biker. Jon did not pay much attention to the speaker.

48

He was more interested in who he saw at the back doors.

"And he shall rise up with the army of the damned and have man take responsibility for their sins to the father," said the speaker.

This was very strange. The speaker of the meeting usually shares their experiences with alcohol and drugs. This speaker was out of the ordinary. His voice no longer had a Boston accent but more like a southern preacher's voice. He started to get louder. The other members started to get uncomfortable. He walked to the back of the room, asking those he passed if they were 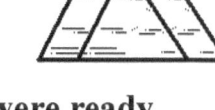 ready for his arrival and if they were ready to repent for their sins.

"And you sir…" he said to Jon. "What will you do when he comes? Will you beg for his mercy and join his side for the sins of mankind? Will you sacrifice yourself for the salvation of mankind?"

Jon paused for a moment. He looked around at everybody in the room. Jon did not want to be bothered. Jon replied,

"I don't believe in God nor do I believe in salvation. I won't need to beg for a damn thing!"

The room fell silent. Everyone was looking at them. Finally the preacher cracked a smile.

"Honesty!" yelled the preacher to the people. "The man answered me with honesty. So, what does that tell us?"

Then the preacher leaned over to Jon and whispered in his ear with a devilish voice, "You shall see no mercy."

The preacher stood straight up and held a book high above his head. He now had everybody's attention. "This man can be helped!" he announced to everybody. "He is honest. The writings tell us we all can be helped if we are able to be honest. This man knows when to be honest. He knows when he has been beaten. He will be able to lay down his arms and admit defeat. He will know when to start begging for mercy. That is the saving gift of being honest!"

The preacher grabbed a wicker basket from the front table.

"And to move on to our next step, we have a tradition that states we are fully self supportive. I'll pass the collection basket around. Give if you can. If you can't, well, I'll see you in Hell!" The speaker said sarcastically. "Thank you."

As they passed the plate around the room, Jon looked over his shoulder to see if anyone was looking at him. He was going to try and snatch some money from the donation basket.

A bright light flashed out from the back room. No one saw it except Jon. Jon first thought it was a camera flash. Then another flash flickered through the small square windows of the two doors in the back of the room. It flashed like lightning. Jon thought it could be an electrical wire.

Jon missed the collection basket as his thoughts were on the flash of light. "Damn it!" mumbled Jon to himself. "Oh, I'm sorry! Did you want to give something?" asked the man sitting in front of Jon.
"No. I'm o.k." Jon said softly as he did not want to make a scene.

"Hey! Bring the basket back here! This gentleman wants to give something!" yelled the man across the room.

Jon was trying to avoid the basket but they passed it back to him anyway. Everybody was watching. Jon could feel all the eyes on him.

"Yeah, Thanks buddy," replied Jon regretfully. He shook his head in his own disbelief of his life. He peeled a dollar out of his pocket, not letting anyone see how much money he had. He placed the dollar in the basket.

After they took the basket away and everyone's attention went back to the front of the room, Jon stood up and wandered to the very back of the church. At the end of a small hallway was a set of doors. There was no sign of anyone else being back there. The electrical outlets in the hall all looked to be all right. Jon looked inside the small glass window on one of the doors. The room inside was quiet and dark.

Jon slowly walked into the dark filled room. The doors lead him to the storage building in the back of the church. But what caught his attention was a satchel lying in the middle of the floor. It was the only thing that was lit from the moonlight. Jon walked over and picked the bag up off the floor.

 Jon thought,
 "I wonder if there is any money in…"
"Jon!" someone called out. Bill entered through the doors and stood at the entrance. "We're taking a fifteen minute break."
 Jon slipped the satchel into his coat without Bill seeing. Bill looked at Jon with some concern. He slowly walked into the center of the room and turned around.
Bill continued,
"This used to be a burial ground of some sort, before they built the church. Holy land they called it. It started out as a small chapel with one Priest. They say that he knew things that most people didn't know, back then. They say that he could tell a person's path through life with just one look."
  Then Bill looked Jon in the eyes and said to him,
"When all was at the worst in a person's life, he gave them hope and told them things would change." Bill started to walk away.

"I guess everything changes with time, I suppose?

You got to step outside if you want to smoke. A lot of old folk come to this meeting and the smoke easily bothers them. Are you sure you are okay Jon?"

"Yes! I'm just thinking" Jon replied slowly. Bill responded,

"Well, don't think too much. You don't want to be up in that head of yours for too long. They say that idol time is the Devil's playground. Believe me, I know. I understand. Let me know if I can do anything for you." Bill walked outside.

54

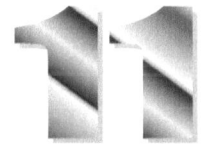

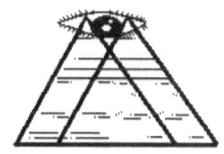

Jon took a moment to gather his thoughts
before returning to the meeting room.
Everyone had gone outside. Jon was left
alone in the church. He wanted to see what
was inside the bag so he started to rummage
through it.
"Jonathan!" Jon thought he heard someone
whisper his name. Did it come from the next
room? Did it come from beyond the two
doors? Was it that freak he had seen

55

earlier? He was not for sure. He thought that he was just starting to hallucinate from the detoxification from heroin. He had just got out of the hospital not long ago and his thoughts were really starting to spin.

Jon wanted to get high. But there was so much to do in order to get a fix. He needed money. The journey he must travel just to get the money was usually gruesome. Lately, things were always hard. He could ask Bill for a couple of bucks.

"That old timer should have enough sympathy to give me some money," he thought. "Or maybe this bag has something of value. Maybe there is something in the satchel that I can trade or sell for money."

Jon didn't want anyone to see him rummaging through the satchel so he headed back through the double doors and into the warehouse building behind the church again.

Jon entered the room and stopped himself quickly. It was dark and this time he did not feel like he was alone. Jon lit his lighter to see what was inside the satchel. The only thing in the bag was a book.

"Damn it!" Jon said. "There isn't anything here. A book! What the fuck do I need a book for? I'm going to have to…" Jon was interrupted.

The doors from the other room had opened. The people started to return to the meeting. Jon quickly stashed the satchel under a table. He walked out the double doors and into the hallway. The bathroom door was to his right so Jon quickly dashed into the bathroom before anyone could see him.

Once inside the bathroom, he wedged open a window with a piece of wood so he could sneak back into the building later on.

Jon walked out of the bathroom and headed towards the front doors. The last person coming in from the break was Bill. "Where are you going Jon?" Bill asked. "I got to go Bill. I got this thing I got to do. Do you know what I mean?" Jon asked rhetorically.
Bill said to Jon,
"Yes, I do, Jon. Well, if you get stuck tonight, I usually leave this door unlocked. Just for cases like this. This house has

always been a helping house with open doors. Who am I to change that? There are blankets and a pillow on a shelf in the back."

Jon walked out the doors and turned around to face Bill.

"Thanks Bill," said Jon.

"Take care tonight," Bill replied and then closed the door.

Later that night, Bill let out the last of the people from the meeting. He shut off the lights and closed the doors in front of him. He left them unlocked like he promised Jon earlier. When he shut the doors, the two A.A. symbols formed on the doors. The symbols had been on the front doors for a long time. They were something that Bill had seen a thousand times before. But tonight, Bill just stood and stared into the symbols. The top of the triangle kept his attention the most. It seemed as if something was looking back at him. Something from beyond was looking in and looking for something.

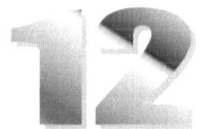

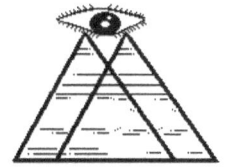

Mark and Doug went to the fence to meet
Dylan. The boys stood outside the fence for
at least an hour. Dylan never showed up.
They were debating on going into the old
abandon building that's connected to the old
church or wait longer for Dylan. The door
swung open on the church side.
"Shush! Get down!" said Doug.
The door to the church had swung opened.
It was the people leaving the meeting. The

59

boys watched from afar as Bill stared at the doors.

"What is he doing?" asked Doug.

"Shush! Wait. Okay. He's leaving," said Mark.

Finally, the boys decide to go in.

Doug had taken a set of bolt cutters from his shed. He took them earlier when he had arrived home from school and put the cutters into his backpack.

Doug made with his bolt cutters. The boys crawled through the hole in the fence. Once they got past the fence they had to walk across a dirt lot for about 20 yards. They kept low and tried to hide behind the over grown weeds. They got to the building and found the back doors had been boarded up.

"What are we going to do now?" Mark asked Doug.

"Don't worry!" Doug assured Mark. "I always come prepared." Doug pulled out a crow bar and a claw hammer from his backpack.

"This shouldn't take long. Let's get to work," said Doug as he stripped off the first piece of wood.

"Quiet down Doug! You're going to get us caught!"

Mark exclaimed about all the noise Doug was making. It did not take long to get in. He was done in less than 30 seconds. The door way was clear and the boys stepped inside.

"Board that back up" Doug said to Mark. Mark got a piece of wood and the old, bent nails and started putting up the boards. "Make sure you put them up good," said Doug. "We don't need any visitors tonight."

But Mark was not handy with a hammer. Some of the boards came loose and fell off after he turned around.

The boys entered the main room. Mark slapped Doug in the back of the head and began to run. Mark used his flashlight to see as the boys ran up a staircase. The stairs were on the far left side of the room and curved up to the balcony that overlooked the room. At the top of the staircase there were three doors on the balcony's floor. The boys went into the middle room.

61

Once inside the room the boys caught their breath. Then they started to go through their inventory. The boys brought an electric lamp, sleeping bags and some food.

Mark had a list of things that they might find tonight. The real fun was walking around in the dark in an old abandon building with a flashlight. The boys loved adventure.

An old brush and mirror set, a safe, any type of a weapon, a pair of glasses, a satchel, a hat, gloves and a crucifix were some of the items on the list for tonight's treasure hunt.

Mark told his parents that he was sleeping over Doug's house. And Doug told his parents he was sleeping over Marks house. They think they have everything covered for tonight's exploration. They were even going to map out some of the secret passages that were rumored to be underneath the building of an old church. Tonight was going to be the most exciting night of their life. They did not know how right they were!

13

Jon walked the night down the city street that he knew so well. These streets have been his home for some time. It's easy to get here but there's no easy way out. The streets were vacant. Not a person in sight. All of the stores were closed. There were hardly any cars. The cars that were there were abandoned. All of the row houses had bars on their doors and windows. Trash blew around like tumbleweed in a ghost town and graffiti defaced everything that once had beauty. These are the poor streets of Philadelphia.

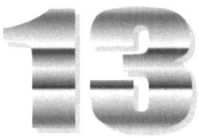

Jon knows how beautiful this city can be. The streets he grew up on were clean and peaceful. The kids use to play stickball in the street while the elderly sat in the park and played chess. Now, the broken down streets are the gaming grounds for the drug addicted and poverty stricken. Those who play know these gaming grounds as being "Down the Way".

Jon sees people who are doing wrong in order to survive. The drug culture is quick money for bread and a pack of diapers. He knows the neighborhood needs a new beginning. He hopes he could change it one day. He wants to be able to help one day. But tonight, Jon is only thinking about one thing, himself. Jon is only thinking about his pain. He just wants to numb himself out.

Jon usually mixed his fix right after buying heroin off the street. He would go into the first abandon house he saw and mix up his stuff. Then, by using the moonlight to see, he got himself off. This was normal for Jon.

Jon continued walking. He turned into a vacant lot with an abandon house next to it. He walked to the back of the abandon house.

"Dope! Dope!" Jon shouted softly towards the second floor of the abandon house. Somebody appeared at the top floor window. The window was partially boarded with old boards. They are not any boards the city would have put up. The dealers made it for their protection. The dealers lowered a coffee can down a rope through a loose board. Jon put his money in the can.

"One" said Jon.

The drug dealer pulled up the can with the money in it.

A few seconds later, the can came back with one bag of heroin in it. Jon grabbed the bag from the can and turned around. A boy was standing right behind him. Jon was startled.

"Would you give up a life?" said the boy but Jon thought he must have heard him wrong.

"What?" asked Jon bewildered?

"Would you give up a light? Holmes." The boy asked again while twirling a cigarette. The kid could not be any older then twelve years old.

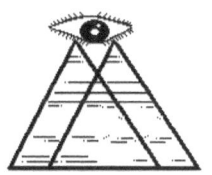

"Next time you come down here for your fix, come find me. I got some shit that will rock your world!" the boy told Jon.

"Yeah, sure kid. I'll look for you" Jon replied while lighting his cigarette.

"You bet your life you will!" a deep, dark voice answered Jon. Jon lifted his eyes to look at the little boy but nobody was there. It was if the boy had vanished. Or maybe he didn't even exist at all. Jon was confused. He looked down at the stamp on the bag of heroin and the exact lettering was "YOUR LIFE".

Jon started walking to the first abandon house he usually went to, to get high.

Jon had not used any drugs for five days. He was trying to talk himself out of getting high. But his addiction knew how to weaken Jon. Images of all the reasons for him to get high flashed through his mind. Jon's body was still going through some physical detoxification as well. Jon did not want to hurt anymore. Jon now had his bag of heroin in his hand. There was no stopping. He was going to end his pain, for a moment.

Jon went down an alleyway to get to the abandon house. As he got closer, he saw that the back door was newly boarded up. The housing authority was there earlier. They boarded all the entrances. There was no easy way inside.

Jon thought to himself for a minute, "Shit! Think Jon! Think! It's okay. I'll just go to the next abandon minimum (street slang for an abandon house used to shelter addicts and the homeless) I used to sleep in. That house has better light in it anyway. I can see myself hit a vein better. I can hold off for a few minutes." Jon huffed his way to the next house.

As he walked down the street it started to get very windy. A gust of wind blew past and almost knocked Jon onto the ground.

In the far skies, lightning struck every few seconds. A thunderstorm was forming. Jon continued on to the next abandon house. He knew he would need some shelter. With that kind of wind, it will blow his heroin all over the place when trying to prepare it. This was the only little bit of heroin that Jon could afford. He could not afford to spill any. Jon had to make this shot count and hit his main vein without any mistakes.

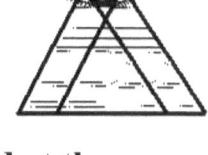

Jon turned the corner and looked at the abandon house he was heading to. There was a fallen tree right in the middle of the house. People from the neighborhood were outside looking at the tree.

"Oh, no!" said Jon angrily to himself. He mumbled something to himself as if he was trying to catch a thought that flashed in between all his other thoughts.

Jon could hear the neighbor in the background talking, "Yea, it was like this huge gust of wind came from around that corner and wrapped itself right around that tree."

Jon was talking hysterically at himself. "What now? Where can I go now? I wonder if anybody is at the church. After all, the guy did offer for me to spend the night. He doesn't have to know I'm high. No one will know. No one can tell. So who would care? Yea right, there is no one here that cares? There's no one here that cares!"

Jon suddenly felt lonely. He started to whimper and was ready to cry. But Jon stopped his crying abruptly and said to himself,

"No pity for me. No way in hell! No way"

You could tell by his body language that Jon really did not want to hurt anymore. The death of his fiancé and their unborn child was more then he could handle. To him, there was no cure for his pain. It was a scar on his heart. And now the physical dependency to narcotics his body craves is wearing hard on his body.

The pain that he felt emotionally caused him to hurt physically. There was no other pain stronger then what he was already feeling. Jon would do anything to make it stop. Even take lesser pain to forget about his main pain. He would even cut himself. But Jon finally found some relief inside a needle. To Jon, heroin was an immediate relief from his pain and morbid memories.

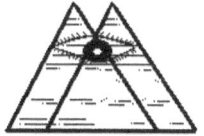

14

Dylan's mom and dad came home from work. Dylan and Jessica were always happy to see their parents. And their parents loved to see them. Their mom and dad always wanted to know everything that Dylan and Jessica learned that day.

What the children loved best about their mom and dad was that they understood. Their parent sincerely listened to what their children had to say. The children respected them for that. They trusted their parents and knew their parents would never bring them any harm.

Their Mom started dinner and their dad checked homework. They all talked about their day. Dylan and Jessica told them about the homeruns they had earlier today. There was no mention of the spiritual connection they shared. Still, it was a happy and pleasant atmosphere. Every night was pretty much the same. After dinner the children washed up and their parents cleaned the dishes. Next, they'll play a board

70

game or watch a movie together. These folks live for the moments they spend together.

Later on, the phone rang and Dylan's mom answered. "Hello! Really?" said his mom in surprise.

"No. They're not here. I have not seen them all night." Dylan's mom said into the phone.

"Dylan!" his mom called for Dylan.

"Yeah" Dylan said entering the room.

"Have you seen or heard from Mark or Doug? It's Marks mother on the phone and she said that Mark was suppose to sleep over Doug's. Well, Doug's mom called over Mark's house asking to talk to Doug and they weren't there. Nobody knows where Mark and Doug are. Do you know where they are?" She asked Dylan.

"No mom. I have not seen them since school." Dylan replied. His mom relayed what Dylan said to her and then hung up the phone. Dylan's mom looked at her son and then gave a sarcastic smile. She knew Dylan knew something. She was happy that it wasn't him doing the sleep outs. Mom was grateful to have been blessed with two fabulous children.

71

15

The boys were all set up in the middle room on the top floor. They had their sleeping bags and a battery-operated lamp that kept the room well lit. The boys laid out a diagram (map) of the building and church. Mark had made it up earlier that day at school. Marks dad worked for a construction company and he always had access to blueprints and graph paper. The layout he had made looked professional.

Mark and Doug figured that if there were any kind of secret tunnels they would be in the basement between the church and the building.

"Well, it looks like we'll be heading to the basement. Grab the flashlights Doug." Mark ordered Doug, "and grabs the list of treasures." Doug was defiantly stronger

72

then Mark but Doug respected Mark. He knew Mark was just teasing him. But, there did have to be a leader on this journey. Mark did have better knowledge of the area. "Let's go!" said Doug. He grabbed his overloaded backpack, the flashlights and the list of treasures.

"What do you have in the back pack? You're going to need all the room you can for the treasures you find. You idiot!" said Mark.

Doug replied,

"What every journeyman should bring with him on his journeys: a rope, a knife, waterproof matches, and a bottle of water. What are you bringing?" Mark was stunned by Doug's answer, which left Mark speechless and feeling a little embarrassed.

"Let's go!" said Mark as he grabbed a flashlight and a bottle of water.

The boys walked out of the room and onto the balcony. The stairs were to the right of them. It was dark. The only light was the moonlight that barely seeped in from a small covered window above the exit doors. The boys turned their flashlights on. They walked to the edge of the railing and shined their flashlights around the room. To the left, on the ground floor were the two doors that led to the inside of the church. The doors were the same doors that Jon went through earlier. There was some furniture and an oval mirror near the doors. Towards the center of the room all they could see was the hard wood floors from the moonlight. But, when they looked up, there was a black iron rod and a wooden chandelier right in front of them. The boys found a wench nearby and swung the chandelier over to them. It did not light with electricity. Its light only came from candles.

"Let's light it up!" said Mark. But before he could finish his last words, Doug had already lit a match and lit one of the candles on the chandelier. A circle of candles sporadically caught flame and the chandelier began to self-ignite. In seconds, the chandelier brightly lit the entire room. Once the room was completely lit, the light unveiled a room that left the boys star struck.

   On every wall and every indentation around the room, many different types of ancient weapons became visible. The weapons were from different cultures from different times in earth's history. The weapons shined when they reflected the light from the chandelier. Their metal shine enlightened the room even more.

Underneath the staircase was a large round table that had a mid evil logo in the center. "I wonder how old this stuff is?" asked Mark. "I've never seen so many weapons before!" He exclaimed. "WOW! Look at this Mark. It's some kind of samurai sword or something? Over here on this wall, it's some kind of native spears. There are weapons all over!"

"We didn't see them when we first came in because we didn't have any light and we ran straight to the room," said Mark.

"This is amazing!" the boys exclaimed. "You're going to have to get a bigger bag," said Mark. They both laughed.

"Doug, go make sure all the doors are locked," Mark told Doug. "Make sure you lock all the doors."

They both headed down the winding stairs
and Doug ran off to lock all the doors in the
church.

   All sorts of ancient weapons hung along
the wall of the staircase.

   "We can't take all of these weapons," said
Mark to himself doubtfully. "I mean, it
looks like somebody might notice them
missing. And how are we going to carry all
these swords and things anyway?"

   Doug returned from locking the doors.
"Hey guys. It's an odd thing. The front
doors to the church were unlocked." said
Doug.

"Who the hell would leave the door
unlocked with all this stuff in here?" asked
Mark.

"Obviously, people who trust too much,"
said Doug as he walked over to a table. He
swiped the blanket off the table it was
covering. He laid the blanket on the floor
and opened it up flat.

"Don't worry. We're not going to take
everything!" assured Doug. "Get what you
think is most valuable and we'll wrap them
up in this cover. We'll only take a couple of
things and come back next week. If it looks

like no one was here then we'll take the rest of the stuff."

"Sounds good to me," agreed Mark.

The boys grabbed a couple of swords from the walls. Mark found a crossbow that carried silver tipped arrows. Doug found a shield and started to load it up with weapons. Doug found a crucifix that turned into a sword and a blade formed when you detached the body of Christ for double-blade action.

The boys couldn't help to notice that all of these weapons were religious in some sort of way.

"Do you think we'll go to hell for this?" asked Mark. He then tried to justify his wrong doings by saying, "I mean it's not technically the church. It's the building behind the church. And these are weapons. And weapons are for war. There is nothing religious about war. So, we are not really steeling from God. Not really! Is that right Doug?"

Doug replied,

"Well, it doesn't really matter to me. There's treasure here right now. And I am a treasure hunter. If God did not want us to have this stuff then he would have never let us find it.

Besides, it might be my treasure from my past life." The boys both had a laugh.
  They continued to search around the room for more treasures. They felt along the walls and the floors to see if there were any secret passages. Doug crawled on the floor and spotted something underneath a table that was near the doors that lead to the church. "I found something, treasure" Doug announced to Mark. "It looks like a leather book bag! That is one point for me." "Man, you're finding everything tonight. You're on fire!" said Mark. "Check it off the list!"
  Doug set the tan leather satchel down on the floor. He loosened the straps and opened the flap. At first, there was a red glow coming from inside the bag. What Doug pulled out next was amazement to both of their eyes. It was something that this world has never seen before and no human eyes have ever looked upon.
  It was a book. Not just any book. Doug could tell right away that this book was not

78

just an average book. He was very cautious as he lifted it out of the satchel. On the front cover was a circle. Inside the circle, images kept appearing. Doug was memorized. An image of a star appeared. Suddenly, the star went up in a blaze! Doug pushed the book to the center of the floor.

"Whoa! Hey Mark? Mark! Mark!"

Mark slowly walked over towards Doug. "What is it Doha…?" Mark was dumbfounded by what he saw.

A 3-D holographic image projected above the cover of the book. It was a shadowy image of a person.

Mark said,

"That image, is that Dylan? It looks like …"

"Ka-boom!" Thunder suddenly roared through the house. A burst of wind blew in through the back doors blowing out all the candles. Everything went dark.

16

Jessica abruptly entered into Dylan's room and took him by surprise.

"You're not going to do what I think you are? Are you?" Jessica asked Dylan. Dylan was putting his sneakers on his feet.

"What do you mean?" Dylan responded.

"You know what I mean. You're going to meet with Doug and Mark," said Jessica.

"I just want to let the guys know that their parents are looking for them so they can get their story straight when they get home. It's still early enough for them to go home and say they went to the mall or something. So they won't get in any trouble." Dylan said.

"So, you do know where they are?" Jessica asked.

Dylan responded,

"Look, just cover for me. They went to the old church building to look for treasure. I'll be right back. I promise."

"Okay, as long as you promise me that you will come right home after you find them. Don't take all eternity to get back. Please be careful. I don't like it when you're not here." Jessica said to Dylan.

"I'll be as fast as I can. Trust me Jessica, I'll be okay." Dylan had assured her. He opened his bedroom window and stepped out onto the roof. Dylan was able to step into the tree hanging over the roof of his house. He climbed down the tree and ran off into the woods.

17

The book lay in a circle in the center of the room.
A 3-D hologram of a door had appeared above the books' cover. It memorized the boys. It was very mystical.
"Whoa! We better get out of here. This stuff is not ours to be messing with," said Mark.
"Slow down brown stain. There's nobody here and nobody is coming here tonight," replied Doug.
Mark replied, "Exactly! No people, no help! That equals me with a brown stain in my shorts!"
The boys laughed at the sarcasm.
"Look, inside the flame above the book!" Doug exclaimed.
There was a picture of two kids standing inside a circle that was marked out on the floor. The circle lit up with changing colors.
"The picture looks like what is going on right now with us!" exclaimed Mark.

"I think it's trying to tell us something," said Doug.

"Listen! Can you hear it?"

Mark and Doug moved closer to the book. "Is there somebody standing in the doorway?" asked Doug. A set of red glowing eyes appeared in the dark shadows of the door.

"HELP ME!" a deep dark voice spoke aloud.

Mark and Doug became instantly entranced. They were now under the control of the powers from within.

A pentacle star set a blaze inside the circle where the boys stood. The boys did not move. They stared into the doorway with a blank face as the fire wrapped itself around their bodies. Both of the boy's eyes filled with total blackness and the flames acted as chains that held them prisoner. Flames began to rise higher around the room. The book's cover burned bright but remained undamaged. It appeared that the whole room was on fire. The flames may have not damage the book, but it was "Hot as Hell" in the room.

18

Jon finally reached the church doors. He tried to open the doors but they were locked.

"Thanks a lot, Bill!" said Jon to himself sarcastically. Jon was still desperate to get high. He needed to get his fix right away. He walked over to the bathroom window on the side of the church. It was still opened from the piece of wood that he put there earlier. "Well, this is it!" he thought. "After I climb in the window then it becomes a crime. At least I'll be high."

That is all that mattered to Jon. Five days off of the heroin and his mind is still going crazy.

Jon didn't hesitate to try and climb in the window. He quickly realized the window was too high from the ground for him to get inside. Jon set a trashcan upside down and stood on it to reach the bathroom window. He could barley reach the ledge of the window and the wind was blowing really hard. But Jon did not have any sense of the common man. He was thinking irrationally.

After Jon grabbed the ledge of the window a gust of wind blew the trashcan out from underneath him. Jon hung on to the window ledge before finally pulling himself up. Jon pulled himself into the window and fell fast to the ground, hitting the floor on the other side. There was a five-foot drop to the floor. Jon hit the floor hard. He twisted his wrist and ankle and had a short black out. Jon did not let it bother him for too long. He was now inside with some shelter. There were more important matters at hand. Jon could now mix up his heroin.

Jon shook off his dizziness. He leaned over to the sink and pulled himself up. He needed a couple of drops of water to mix the heroin. Jon turned the knobs on the sink but no water came out.

"No water! The water must be turned off," he thought.

Jon could not stand anymore so he fell back down onto the bathroom floor. He turned the knobs underneath the sink. Still no water came out. Not one drop! Jon was so desperate to get high. All he needed were a few drops of water to mix up his drugs. After all he has been through so far tonight and now he is just a few drops of water short of reaching his reward.

He felt all the weight of his life's defeats crashing on top of him. Jon closed his eyes and slid his body down onto the floor. Jon started to mumble,
"I don't want to live anymore. Why do you keep me alive? Why?"

Jon laid face down on the floor. Jon's eyes opened and he found himself staring at the bottom of a toilet bowl. Jon no longer wanted to get high but he needed to get high. It was not so much for his physical pain but more for him to regain his sanity. Jon's mind would not stop craving. Then, Jon had an idea. He sat himself up and dragged himself over to the toilet bowl.

87

There was still some water in the bottom of the toilet.

Jon only needed a small amount (20 units) of water to mix up his heroin. The toilet bowl looked pretty clean and the water was clear, not yellow like someone urinated in it. He had only heard of people using their urine to shot up their drugs. Jon doesn't believe it's true, but then again, here he is looking down the bottom of a toilet bowl. Jon was afraid to flush the toilet because the water might not fill back up. Jon felt alone, cold, tired, and indeed desperate.

"It's time to feed the dragon!" mumbled Jon out loud.

Jon stuck his needle into the toilet bowl and drew up 20 units of water. He opened the bag of heroin and emptied all of the powdery substance onto a metal spoon. The powder was an eggshell white color. He then took the needle and pushed the water into the spoon with the powdery substance. Jon quickly mixed the two together using the plunger of the needle to stir them together. He used his lighter to light the bottom of the spoon. The mix quickly came to a simmer. The odor from the cooking rose to Jon's

88

nose. Jon loves that smell. He was almost there. Jon bit off a piece of his cigarette filter. He rolled it into a tiny ball and dropped it into the heroin mix. He was using it in place of a piece of cotton. It was used to filter out any cut or tiny objects that would clog in his needlepoint. Using the cigarette filter is known as "the poor man's cotton". He stuck the needle into the "cotton" and pulled back on the needles' plunger. It sucked up whatever liquid that was on the spoon. Once inside the needle, the mix turned a clear light brown color. That was the color of really strong heroin, in Philadelphia. Jon has not done any heroin for a couple of days and is aware of how low his tolerance is for opiates.

 Over and over again Jon's thoughts were telling him, "It's time to feed the dragon!"
 He was hoping that by mixing up the whole bag that it would take him out forever. "Will suicide be the answer for me?" thought Jon. "No. It is just an addict getting beat by his master."

Jon lifted the syringe so that the needle was on top. He tapped on the syringe until all the air bubbles that were in the mix rose to the top. He then pushed the plunger slowly upwards until all the air bubbles were out of the mix.

"Locked and loaded!" said Jon in the most serious tone.   Without any hesitation Jon rolled up his sleeve, tapped out a vein, and stuck in the needlepoint. He stuck the needlepoint right into the middle of the track mark already on his arm. Abscesses, scar tissue, and soars ran in lines all over his arms. Once the needle was in his vein, he drew back on the plunger. A gush of red blood mixed with the heroin inside the needle's chamber. For Jon, this point was a high in itself. Jon took a deep breath and time seemed to stop. Everything fell silent. A small amount of inner peace entered Jon's mind because he knew what was about to happen. Nothing else mattered to him.

Jon pushed the plunger down into the belly of the needle and the mix rushed into his vein. The rush was instant and fluttered through his whole body. Jon's pupils instantly shrunk to the size of a pin's head.

All of Jon's muscles tightened and gave him strength. He felt indestructible. After the first wave of the rush came pleasure. A sense of satisfaction and ease fluttered Jon. Finally, Jon just sat on the floor and nodded-out as the rest of the mix ran through his body. Now, Jon was numb. Now, Jon felt no pain. Now, Jon felt safe. For now, Jon was resting in peace.

91

19

Dylan climbed through the hole in the fence and headed to the building behind the church. He knew Mark and Doug were already here because he could see their footprints in the mud. Dylan was hoping they didn't go to the passages yet. He felt a little bad that he didn't meet up with Mark and Doug earlier. But then if he did, he would be getting in trouble with them right now. Dylan thought about how his family would react if they found out he was missing. He thought about how frantic everyone might be. Then he thought about if

he were dead. What would his funeral be like? Would there be a line down the street of people paying their respects to him? Or would there only be a hand full of people? Would anyone cry? Would anyone really miss him? Will he be remembered or forgotten? Then Dylan asked himself the question,
"What will they remember me for?"
  Dylan looked above the church building. The skies over top of the buildings were dark gray and formed a swirling vortex. A black hole formed at the end of the vortex. Dylan had a knack for picking up atmospheric vibes. These vibes were all giving him red flags and warning signs that something bad was about to happen. And he hoped that this had nothing to do with Mark and Doug.

20

The room was completely on fire. Everything was burning except where the boys stood, inside the circle. It appeared that Mark and Doug were under some kind of trance. Mark and Doug would read something from the book in a creepy language and then they would write something on the floor. Each time they wrote down a symbol on the floor, the circle would flash and the ground would rumble.

Dylan entered through the back of the building where Mark and Doug had entered earlier and the wind had blown open the doors. He saw the whole room was a blaze. "What the Hell!" Dylan exclaimed.
Doug looked up at Dylan. Dylan looked into Doug's eyes and saw they were completely black. He said to Dylan with a demon like voice,
"It will be done! Open the gates book keeper!" Doug turned away and continued writing on the floor.

Dylan could not believe what he was seeing. He ran over to the fire extinguisher and took it off the wall. He removed the safety latch and began to spray the fire in the center of the book. "No!" A cry came from inside the book as it started to distinguish out. It seemed that the whole room would extinguish as the book's flames went out. Dylan sprayed the rest of the area with the fire extinguisher. Smoke formed everywhere as the white extinguishing foam smothered the fire. Mark and Doug broke out of their trance.

95

They were screaming and crying as they ran out the double doors. The hairs on their heads were singed.   Once the boys got outside they looked back at the old church building and noticed the black hole overhead. "What is that?" asked the boys. "What in the Hell is that? Let's get out of here!" The boys ran away.

  The fire was just about out. The circle in the center of the room was still shinning bright. The book lied open in the middle of the circle. Above the book was a hologram of a door. The single door was swaying with the wind. A light was coming from the inside of the door. And then Dylan heard a voice. "What?" answered Dylan bewildered "Yes, I'll try to help you. Where are you?"

  The voice sounded like a little girl. The sound of her voice was quite pleasant and soothing to hear. It was memorizing, but Dylan was not entranced. It was the care for another person that led Dylan to walk through the door above the book. Dylan's mind was strong. His body was healthy. Bravery and courage sat on each of his shoulders. But for this task Dylan knew he needed a lot more than that.

Dylan made the sign of the cross and stepped through the door. His body disappeared as he stepped through the opening. When Dylan stepped through the doorway and into the other side there seemed to be no change. He was in the same room he was just in. He turned around and looked through the doorway and saw the same room. Suddenly, a gust of wind blew through the front doors where Mark and Doug had run out. The gust of wind slammed the holographic door closed with Dylan still inside. Everything nearby instantly got sucked into the book as the book spun violently around and finally slammed shut. Everything went dark!

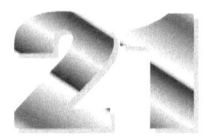

Jon's Dream

Jon lunged forward. But, then he realized it wasn't forward he was lunging. He was lunging upward. He was climbing. Higher and higher he climbed.

"What am I climbing?" asked Jon out loud to himself. He could see it was white and as wide as his body.

"I must have wings. I am climbing upward and something from behind me keeps thrusting me higher and higher. I must have wings? Am I almost to the top?" Jon thought to himself as he kept lunging forward. The only sound he could hear was his breathing.

Finally, he made it to the top. He had climbed to the top of a tall, white marble pillar that stood in the middle of nowhere. Total darkness surrounded Jon. There was only a one-foot long square ledge on top of the pillar to rest on.

"I'll stand for awhile. Then I'll fly again," said Jon in a crazy minded way. Then Jon thought he better sit to get better rest. He sat on top of the pillar, dangling his legs over the edge. He looked into the distance. At first he realized he was alone and got a little scared.

"Where am I going to fly next?" This question flashed through his mind a thousand times. Then he saw something afar.

"Is that, I think it is. It's another pillar," said Jon to himself. There was another pillar.

"I must go from pillar to pillar to get to the golden gates?" Further still Jon could see another pillar.

In the far, far away distance Jon could see a faint light that had a golden glow.

"That must be where the gates of heaven are!" Jon thought. "That is where I must go. They may be there."

The other pillars were real far away. He didn't remember how he got his wings but he was sure he could fly. Jon crouched down to take a mighty leap. Just as he was about to lunge, two thunderous cracking sounds came from behind Jon. The sounds were fearsome and made him scared and then Jon felt pain. His white wings had cracked at the bone connected to his back. As Jon turned around, both of his wings fell from his shoulder blades and twirled down into the darkness until they were seen no more. "No!" cried Jon.

The pillar top became too slippery for him to stand on. Jon carefully sat down. "What am I going to do now? The pillars look so far away," said Jon as he sat there covered in his own blood. The pillars were too far away. Time had passed and the pillars faded into the distance. So much time has passed and Jon just sat there with absolutely no contact with anyone. Not even a breeze from wind blew by.

Jon started to lose his mind. So many times he had thought about just jumping into the black hole. Would it be a leap of faith or suicide?

Jon had seen nothing for a very long time. Then, "What is that?" exclaimed Jon. A dim light had appeared in the distance. It was a light in which he has not seen in a long time, or so he thought. It was the same light that he thought was the gates of heaven before. To Jon, this little light was hope. It is the light that ignites inside of us during our darkest hour.

"Is it someone who could help me? I hope so. I can't stand anymore," said Jon to himself doubtingly. He had been standing there for so long he has had many hallucinations.

"Help!" Jon tried to cry out but his throat was really dry. His words were no louder than a whisper.

Something started to approach from the light. It was gliding from side to side. As it came closer Jon could see its massive wingspan. It appeared to be glittery-white in color. It was one of the most beautiful things Jon has ever seen. The wings were pure white feathers with a silvery shine. It looked like it was sent from heaven with its shining silver lining. The wings pushed for speed. When the wings connected overhead they made a heavenly symbol. At least that is what Jon saw. Jon was truly enlightened by the beauty of these wings.

"What kind of animal do these wings give flight to?" Jon asked himself.

Jon could not see what was underneath the wings.

Jon was getting excited. He could see the Gates of Heaven getting brighter in the distance.

"Maybe, they have sent an angel to come help me," thought Jon.

"Never leave a fallen man behind."

Jon gave a quick thought of how honorable he used to be when he was in the military. Suddenly Jon saw red lights beaming from the gates. Jon looked up to find the winged creature right in front of him. The beast quickly tackled Jon off the pillar. They both plummeted into the darkness. Jon managed to get a glimpse of the creatures face. Fearful black eyes and sharp pointy teeth

102

stared back at Jon as they fell
uncontrollably into the darkness.

   Jon sat up quickly and bumped his head
underneath the bathroom sink. He was
covered in sweat.
"That was one crazy dream!" said Jon out
loud.
   The bathroom light overhead was
flickering on and off. It was bothering his
eyes. He stood up and leaned over the sink.
He turned the water on and splashed some
water on his face. He got a paper towel and
started to dry his face and hands. Then he
paused.
"Wait a minute. Now the water works?" Jon
said to himself as he walked over to the sink
and turned on the water.
"This is fucking weird!" said Jon in
disbelief. But something didn't feel right. He
freshened up and began to walk out the
bathroom door. He stopped at the doorway
and looked back. He noticed that the
window he had climbed through earlier had
been shut and locked.

"How the fuck did that happen? Is somebody here with me? Maybe it was Bill?" thought Jon.

He walked out of the bathroom.
He walked into the room where the meeting had been held. It was dark and quiet. Nobody was around and all the chairs were missing. There was no carpet either but Jon didn't pay much mind.

22

A noise came from the back room. It sounded like something got knocked over. Jon went into the back room to see what it was.

It was dark. He could hear something wrestling around in the far corner. Whatever it was struck fear into Jon. He knew something was not right.

Jon remembered the bag he had hidden earlier. Jon bent down to get the bag from under the table. "Hush!" a noise came from underneath the table. Jon saw a little boy curled up underneath the table holding onto a book. "What are you…?" Jon started to say but was silenced when the boy put his finger over Jon's mouth. The boy pointed over to the corner. It was completely dark. Then the boy quickly shined his flashlight into the corner where the noises were coming from. The light shined on a beastly looking being.

105

Its back was toward them. They could tell it had human characteristics but could not believe it could possibly be human. It looked human as far as arms, legs and body. It had long, stringy hair like straw. It wore round, dark tinted goggles around its eyes. It wore a torn garment, which covered only part of its body. The color of its skin was gray like rotten meat. It kept talking to itself. Its voice had a wheezing sound when it spoke to itself.

The boy made room for Jon to join him. Jon joined him without any hesitation. Jon took notice to the book that the boy was holding onto.

"What is that thing?" Jon whispers to the boy.

Dylan lifted his hand and pointed his finger to a passage in the beginning of the book. It read…

… At the doors of each way, a greeter will be. They will not harm you if harmful you are not. Once they fulfill their destiny, redemption shall be theirs… Jon looked at Dylan. Dylan shrugged as if he didn't know what to do. Jon figured he was the oldest so he better do something first.

"It said it won't hurt us, right?" asked Jon.
"Whatever you say mister," Dylan whispered back.
"Call me Jon" replied Jon.

Jon grabbed a tin cup that had been lying on the floor. The beast had been scrimmaging through a pile of boxes. Jon threw the cup over to the opposite side of the room to see the creature's reaction. The cup made a loud clanking sound.

"What? Who's there? Is somebody here? Are you here? Boy? Boy? I've been waiting for you," said the beastly looking animal. It appeared to have an old female voice.

Jon looked over at Dylan and told him to stay hidden. It appears the beast has a hard time with sight.

"What boy?" Jon had asked.

"So, someone is here. You must be the Guardian," said the creature as it walked into the light. The creature showed itself as a woman. She was deformed maybe, but not a woman of full figure.

"Guardian?" asked Jon.

"Yes. I am only here to meet one person. But that one person travels with a guardian. That would be you," said the creature. "Where's the boy?"

"The boy is safe. You can talk to me," said Jon.

"Fool!" yelled the old lady. "Do you even know where you are? If he is in here, he is safe, if not in here, and then safe he is not! They know he's coming. That's all they know. But soon they will know where and surround this holy land and allow nothing to leave. Not until they have what they want!"

The old lady hissed as she wandered around the room. She was throwing some kind of dust in the air.

Jon said to her, "Okay lady, first of all, who are they? Who are you? And what do you mean where am I? I know where I am, lady. Do you know where you are? I think you are a little crazy!"

"You will have your day Guardian. You will have your day." The old lady said freakishly.

"What's that supposed to mean?" asked Jon in anger.

The old lady replied,
"No more. It is not you I am destined for. I can not rest until I finish my service."
"You better tell me…" Jon started to say but the old lady interrupted him. "No more talking to you! I need to finish what I am doing. Go get the boy if he's still alive and bring him here!" She demanded. "You better hope he's safe. What kind of Guardian are you? You better find the boy!"
"Who are they?" asked Dylan as he stepped out from under the covered table.

23

  The old lady walked over to Dylan. She looked him over from top to bottom. She squeezed his arms and even sniffed him to check his smell. Finally she said,
"Ah! The boy! Yes, yes! Come, over here boy, let me look at you! You look so alive. Full of life."
"Do I know you?" asked Dylan. "And why did you sniff me?"
After a brief pause and then she responded, "The demons, they smell funny. And as for you, no Dylan, you don't know me. But I know who you are. And you are very special."
She stepped back from Dylan and continued to talk.

"There is something you need to know before you go."

"Go! Go where?" asked Dylan.

"To the Holy Land!" responded the old lady.

  Jon started to get fidgety. He did not want to go too far away. He is going to need another fix.

"What! What Holy land? Why? This is crazy!"

"Not for you to ask," said the old lady.

"Get the hell out of here! I'm leaving. This is some kind of crazy bullshit! And lady, I feel real sorry for whatever happened to you, but I got my own bullshit I can't deal with!" Jon huffed his way to the front doors.

"Jon, don't go!" said Dylan.

The old lady yelled,

"There is something you don't know Guardian! You don't know where you are! You are in hell!"

Jon yelled back, "Tell me something I don't know!" Jon stormed out the front doors and the doors slammed shut behind him.

"Jon! No! Don't go!" Dylan ran over to the doors and quickly reopened them.

"No! Dylan! Don't open those doors!" screamed the old lady. But it was too late.

A blast of flames had swung both of the doors wide open and sent Dylan flying back onto the floor.

"Oh, are you all right?" asked the old lady. Dylan stood up. He shook off the blast and looked out the doors. There were flames all around the doorway. The sky was red, the land was made of red desert sand and the trees were dead or in flames. He could see the city buildings burning in the distance. Everything was in ruins or in flames. The sight alone put fear into Dylan and even more so, that Jon was nowhere in sight. It was as if he just vanished once he walked through those doors.

Dylan's first look at hell was overwhelming.

"Where am I?" asked Dylan in a frightened voice.

"Beyond those doors, what you see, that is Hell!" said the old lady as she closed the doors. The old lady spoke calmly to settle Dylan down.

"That is a land of the death. A land where only evil can survive."

"What about Jon?" Dylan asked.

"Your friend stepped into the wrong territory. This is the Devil's realm," she said. "Hopefully, my spell will hide him, but he is weak in his mind right now. He sees what he wants him to see."

It was hard to understand her talking because of her wheezing and her heavy accent.

"The land that we sit on right now is a holy land. It is a piece of land that belongs to heaven or earth. Your lifetime does not have a name for it because it does not exist to your kind. To those who dwell here, it is known as Hell's Earth. It is a piece of land that has been blessed by the divine as a way to …" The old lady paused for a breath and then continued to warn Dylan, "Well that's not important. It is used as a safe haven. In here, in the lighted land, you may stay safe. But, once they find you, and they will find you, the longer you wait, the more of his generals and soldiers will line up and surround this whole holy land and make it impossible to leave."

"Why do I have to go to another Holy Land and not just do it here?" asked Dylan.

She responded with a heavy ascent, "Smart boy you are. This land you must travel. It came from earth. God blessed the land the same time you lived there. The land we are on now is not from your time. Therefore, if you were to return from here you would return to your planets past, and not your present time."

"The Holy Land lies across the dry baron oceans of what you know as the Atlantic and through the volcanic mountains of Ural. Finally, you must travel through the frozen woods of Hell. This is where you must learn to use the book. You will learn how to align each realm with its frequency. You will align them with the stars and with time. Only there, <u>on</u> holy soil, <u>from</u> your time, will the book find the right frequencies to create a passage. You will know! You will know!"

"Home?" asked Dylan as if he were afraid to hear the answer. The old lady replied, "I know you want to see your family. I miss them too. I cannot lie to you. Things will be different when you return. Not by much. Just be aware. The grain of sand must be exactly at that point in time. All the other grains are the same with slightly other

Hell's Earth copyright © 2015 by Pete Trolene
All Rights Reserved

possibilities. If you ever want to see your family, exactly how they were, you must get one of the closest grains of sand of that time of which you left your world. You must also complete your mission."

"What mission?" asked Dylan, curious to her words.

"It is your destiny, child. Why you are here? What brought you here and for what reason? It is the reasoning behind our own reasoning. You were born for so much more. The talents and abilities you have, and have yet to learn are very unique. A great honor you have."

"Honor for what?" responded Dylan sarcastically.

"It is to experience the satisfactions of being in service. To be of *his* service, is an honor. Every life is equally important. We all have our own cause. Every living thing has a purpose, all the way from a tiny bug to a single blade of grass. We all have a life to live. To be responsible is a life worth living.

 You don't have to know everything boy. You know what you need. Everything else is optional. You'll see, boy, you'll see!" The old lady put her face really close to Dylan. Oddly, her face around the big round goggles that she wore did not seem to be old or wrinkled. Her hair was frightfully stringy and balding. But Dylan felt comfortable around her.

She whispered to Dylan, "Each one of us must except their reasoning and fulfill that cause. And everyone who does will find internal peace. This purpose, success or fail, is the peace in our lives. It is the piece that we were missing. You have your own destiny. You have your own beginning and you have your own end. Sadly, most people don't realize how important their lives really are."

"It is not always about one's self, you know? It can't be about yourself but yet you are always there. Ironic, for some it takes for them to almost be destroyed before shinning their inner light. For others, their own destruction is their destiny. They are the ones who must show others how to be strong. They themselves must have pain in order for others to prosper. They too, shall be rewarded. But, I do not know why? I do not need to know. Nor do I need to know

116

everything. We need to remember that it is the now we must always live in. It is now that we have control of. The rest belong to the Gods."

   The old lady chanted as she circled around the room. She said,
"This should throw off his perception of you. He won't know you are here. But only for a little while."
"Who?" Dylan had asked.
"The Devil!" Have you not been listening? Did you forget where you are?"
The old lady had stopped herself from exploding into an angry rage.
"I am sorry. I forgot this is all new to you. It has been so long since I've had any contact with any civilized beings in a while."
Dylan nodded as he accepted her apology.
   The old lady continued,
"As for your friend... I am afraid if his mind is in a weak state then they can alter his perception. Your friend will see what they want him to see. He will see what hell wants him to see?

The spell will protect him from being detected far away. I just hope he does not go anywhere dangerous. And let's just pray he don't bump into any of his generals." The old lady blessed herself as she was saying a prayer. "Not too bright this Guardian is, No?" she sneered.

"What are Jon's chances of returning alive?" asked Dylan.

She answered, "Not a chance in Hell!"

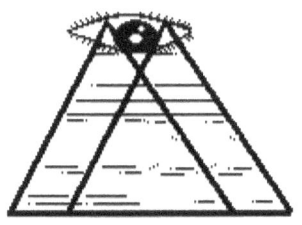

THE DEALER
And
THE DECEIVER

Jon walked down the usual drug trafficking street in Philadelphia. Or so he thought. Things appeared a little different to Jon. There was an alleyway where he usually bought his heroin. It wasn't there. It was the same street he always got his stuff. Something was different. Everything was tranquil. It was dead silent. What scared Jon the most was the fact he had no idea how he got there. It was always a journey to get to the drug streets but now here he was. He doesn't remember how he got there.

The effects from the heroin that he did earlier were wearing off. Withdraw is settling in. His body will start to break down. The effects are like getting an instant flu. Jon thinks he will be sick.

The drugs tell his mind what to think and feel. Jon does not know where he really is. Everything seemed to be spinning around him. He noticed there were no other people around. Surely, somebody would be out hustling on the streets.

A small, broken down, streetlight was the only light in the alley. Jon walked toward the light and passed a couple of trashcans. He heard a noise coming from one of the trashcans. It was a black cat! It hissed and stared him down with its glowing red eyes. Fear struck Jon.

A homeless man was sleeping with his back towards Jon. His heavy moaning and deep breathing had mesmerized Jon for a moment. More fear entered Jon.
Jon never had any fear coming down here before. Jon only worried about cops. They were the only ones who could stop him from

getting a fix. On some days, Jon would pray to get locked up. It was the only way to end his insanity. So why did fear strike now? Cops were the furthest worry for Jon. Why?

Jon continued to walk down the alley. A fog had risen and covered the entire streets and alleyways. He walked right into the fog and the darkness.

"Anyone Out?" asked Jon softly.

"Over here!" a man's voice whispered in the dark.

Jon strained his eyes to see who was there. He could not see anything but darkness. Suddenly, a light flared from the dark corner. It was a match. Jon could smell the sulfur from the after burn.

"What do you desire?" The man asked after he lit his cigarette.

The light from the match went out quickly. All that Jon could see was a guy standing there wearing a cowboy hat and a long trench coat.

"I…I need to get some dope. Are you holding?" uttered Jon.

A snicker came from the man. He said, "I have what you ask. I also have what you Desire! What shall it be?"

"I don't have enough to get your Desire product. Just give me your regular," responded Jon but was unsure of the man's question.

The man was silent for a moment and then chuckled to himself.

Jon was beginning to sweat and get the cold chills. It was time for him to get his next fix.

The dealer puffed on his cigarette. When the cigarette burned bright, Jon could see the dealers face for a quick moment. The dealer's eyes were solid black and he had some scars on his face. They looked like fresh flesh wounds.

Jon had all kinds of bad vibes. And then, the dealer made Jon an offer he could not refuse.

"Here, the first one's on the house." The dealer threw a small light blue bag into the air and it drifted with the wind over to Jon. Jon caught the bag with his hand.

"If you like it, we'll work out a deal."

The hook was in. He had John right where he wanted him. All he had to do was reel him in.

Jon held the bag up to the light. The bag had a red stamp on it that read "DESIRE". Jon saw that there was enough for about one good hit in the bag.

"I guarantee it's the best stuff you ever had. In fact, you can bet your life on it." The dealer said with an arrogant tone. Jon replied,

"Na. Believe me buddy, you wouldn't want my life." The dealer pointed to a door that appeared out of the dark.

"Let's see what you think of your life after you try my heroin. Go right inside that door and get off. No charge. Let me know what you think. You'll have everything you need inside."

Jon walked over to the front of the door. He was hesitant to go in. He stood in front of the door as if he wanted to change his mind.

"What are you waiting for? Go!" demanded the dealer.

Jon pushed the door open and stuck his head inside the doorway.

123

There was a small table and a chair in the center of the room. There was a desk lamp that was tilted down ward to shine light right where Jon would need to see to hit his vein with the needle. The room was small, but the darkness surrounding everything made it appear that the room had no end. Jon took a deep breath and stepped into the room. The door shut behind him. Jon sat down and threw his junk onto the table. "You can bet your life on it," mumbled Jon to himself as he set up the heroin into the spoon. "Hopefully this shit will take my sickness away, or maybe, take me away! For good! Take me away from my own misery."

Jon was all set up. He lifted the syringe and tapped out the air bubbles.

"Here we go."

Jon stuck the needle into his arm. He hit his vein right away. He pulled slightly back on the plunger and the blood gushed into the syringe. The blood mixed with the heroin as if they were meant for each other. With one, slow, steady push of the plunger, the Desire mix rushed into Jon's blood stream. Jon stood to his feet. Jon was instantly taken into a feeling of utter

Hell's Earth copyright © 2015 by Pete Trolene
All Rights Reserved

pleasure, ecstasy and pride. It was the best
rush he had ever felt.
His body instantly raged with heat and
every muscle wanted to explode. Many
people have given their life, their soul and
the lives of all who loved them for such
pleasure.

Jon fell back in the chair as he watched the
room spin around him. He closed his eyes.
This is what he wanted. He felt at peace.

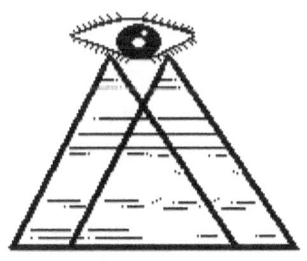

25

"HIGH"

Jon closed his eyes. He began to have a vision.

It started with Jon feeling a rush roll through his body. He was enjoying his high. The smoke in the room spun around him and led Jon into a dream.

126

In his dream, Jon comes into some money. That money led him to more money. That led him to power. He became a very powerful man. He began giving speeches to the people. He would promise riches and good fortune. The people would listen to what he said. He quickly rose to the top of a country. The people loved him. They had parades to celebrate every occasion.

The vision built that country into a strong nation. They were known all around the world.

Jon had promised the people that they would be safe from any intruders. The nation had built a strong army. And they were safe. The people had control of their nation and Jon was at the top.

"To get to the top is one thing. To stay on top is another." **Jon felt the weight of responsibility.**

His people wanted more. They abused what they had and became bored with life's treasures. His nation started to invade their neighboring countries. First, they fought for security. Then, his people wanted to fight for peace. Every battle had an excuse. Every land taken was justified. Every person who died was "needed for the cause." Soon, his nation had blood spilling out from its borders and onto all the surrounding nations. Like a flowing river, his nation's army poured out of its homeland and covered all of the surrounding lands. The army showed no mercy and took no prisoners. Jon's own fame had turned into a dictatorship. His nation had grown so powerful that there was no way to stop them. All of their blood was on Jon's hands. Jon was powerless.

Jon did not like what was happening in his mind. He fought with himself to wake up. He could not wake up out of his daydream. His body rushed with energy but Jon could not move. His body started to convulse. For Jon, it felt really good to be powerful. Now he sits next to death.

Finally, He stopped shaking. Jon came out of his dream. He was drowsy and had foam around his mouth. He rubbed his eyes and opened them slowly. He was surprised he was not in pain. In fact he was in no pain at all. Jon could still feel the heroin running through him.

"Wow! I never did any shit like this before!" said Jon. His voice was tight. He was breathing through his teeth and moving back and forth trying to calm himself. "What the fuck? What the fuck?" Jon said to himself over and over. He was waiting for the heroin to rush out of his body. But it would not stop. His body was stuck in a constant rush. Every two minutes Jon would gasp for air and go right back into the rush.

Jon had found an escape. His mind was on nothing else except the pleasure he was feeling. It was fear in a pleasurable way. Jon felt as if he had escaped into another world. He still does not realize he really is in another world.

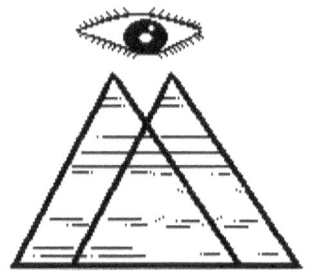

26

Jon stumbled out of the hit house. He could see the city lights on. Their shine, their glow, the rays of light beamed into his eyes. His surroundings were magnificent. The size of the buildings seemed magnified. All the walls of the buildings glittered like crystal; every tree was in full color and danced with Jon as he walked down the street. The stoplight blinked along with the song in Jon's head.

"No, it's not in my head. Everything is able to hear the same music that I here. We all can dance! We all can sing!" said Jon. The trees and the stars, the streetlights and stop signs, they were all dancing with Jon to the beat of the song. Jon was dancing with the world.

"This is awesome!" exclaimed Jon.

Jon fell over some trashcans. He was singing and dancing still. He rolled around in the garbage. He was very intoxicated. He had a bottle of booze in his hand but he does not know how it got there. He felt really drunk. He lay there in the alleyway for a moment. He came to realize he did not know where he was. He looked up at the sky. There were no stars anymore.

"That's strange," said Jon to himself and he began to look around. "There's no moon. Now something isn't right."

There was no light at all in the sky. It was completely black. There was no sound. Not a bird chirped or did a dog bark. Not even the sound of a cricket. Fear once again had struck Jon. He lay there staring at the sky. He was too afraid to move.

Jon was beginning to quickly sober up. He sat up and quickly stood to his feet. He straightened himself up. He took notice that there was only one light lit. It was the same light that was in the alleyway where he met the man in the cowboy hat. Jon was hoping that the dealer was still around.

Jon walked into the darkness and called out for the dealer he had met earlier.

"Yo! Anyone around?" yelled Jon out into the darkness.

There was no response. A feeling of disappointment fell over Jon.

Jon tried again, "Yo! Cowboy! Are you there?"

This time worry filled Jon. He did not want to go through withdraw and detoxify, especially after the powerful stuff he just put into his body.

"So how did you like my product?" asked a voice out of the darkness.

"Oh, you are here? Cool. Well. Yeah, I never did anything like that before!" said Jon.

"Would you like more of my product Jon? I can make you a deal you can't refuse," offered the dealer.

"Sure, but all I have is $10 for now and I'll have to meet up with you tomorrow. I could pay you tomorrow for a front tonight. I you don't know me and all but I'll pay with interest." Jon had begun to get desperate. He tried to bargain with the dealer.

The dealer stood in the dark. He replied, "So, you would like to make a deal? I can make you a deal you can't refuse!"

Jon responded,

"Yeah, yeah, I know. My life! Well, no, I'm not going to give up my life. So, what else are you interested in?"
The dealer replied,
"How about the *boy's* life?"
  All went silent. Jon had another rush of the chills run through his body. Jon thought of the boy and old lady. Images of times when he went through withdraw started to flash in his head again.
"What? What boy?" Jon uttered a response.
  Jon wasn't afraid of the dealer. He was afraid of the pain from withdraw. Paranoid thoughts began to flutter Jon's mind.
"How did he know about the boy? What else does he know? What do I really know? What kind of drugs was I on? Am I still on? Am I hallucinating?"
Jon was now beginning to doubt his surroundings and his own mind.
"Think of it Jon. All the money you could ever dream," said the dealer. "You could have an endless flow of money." A tornado made out of money had formed from behind the dealer and twirled around Jon.
"Anything you wish. A house! Any house you wish!"

The money formed a house around Jon. Then it changed into a cabin, then a horse ranch, overlooking mountaintops, and then a mansion on the beach. It finally ended in a high-class auto dealership.

"Any car you wish Jon. Any color you want. Take the car anywhere you want. Anywhere you would want to escape."

The dealer narrated the show. All sorts of cars and trucks appeared around Jon. All the autos came in many different colors. And each car came with a pretty woman.

"Business, pleasure, fame!" said the dealer. The dealer was conning Jon.

"As for the heroin and booze, the stuff you did earlier, you will have a life time supply, Jon."

"I don't believe this?" said Jon as he put his hands on his head.

"Jon, I am the genie in your lamp. And you just polished your future. What is your wish?" the dealer was trying to deceive Jon. Jon paused for a moment to think. He could not believe what he was hearing.

How did he know about the boy? Does that mean everything the old lady said is true? Everything must be true. And if everything is true then, what the hell did I just stick in my arms?

"Let me get this straight. I get all the riches of the modern world and a life time supply of the best heroin ever, and you want what now?"

"The boy!" yelled the dealer back at Jon. The dealer's voice became monstrous.

 Jon knew it was time to get out of there. "Don't be a fool Jon. Make the deal!" screamed the dealer.

"I...I don't know. Does it have to be that boy? Can it be some other boy? Like, I got this kid on my block, which is such a pain in the ass. He would be great for you. He probably would want to come down here with you."

"Fool! You mach me in my own house!" said the dealer as his voice got very loud and heavy. It was much scarier than the one from before.

"You will die for your disrespect!" said the dealer as he started to grow in body size. He was getting bigger and bigger by the second. He was breathing heavy and grew larger with every breath. He changed into a creature from hell. He is a bounty hunter for the Devil.

The Dealer towered over Jon. A set of wings emerged from his back. The creature stretched out his chest and let out a loud howl.

Jon's surroundings had started to change. The sky had turned from black to red. Thunderclouds and lightning raced across the sky. The buildings were no longer shining. The buildings were broken down and destroyed. The ground turned to red desert sand. The trees were all dead, except the ones that were still burning. A pack of rats were on fire and ran franticly through the streets. You could see the reflection of the destruction, in Jon's eyes.

"Welcome, Jon. Welcome to my home. Welcome to Hell! And this hell is mine!" said the dealer who was now a full-formed demon. He was considered a high spy for the Devil's army. His mission was to retrieve the book and kill the boy and his Guardian.

Suddenly, a blast exploded right in front of the beast. The light from the explosion showed all of the demons evil features. The General had red skin with glowing eyes. He had the tongue of a snake and the teeth of a shark. He had four humungous black horns on his head that were still growing in. The more horns, the higher the ranking, in the Devils army. The General carried six more going down his back. They were all fully-grown.

"Come on Guardian, get in!" A voice shouted from behind Jon. It was Dylan and the old lady. They were driving in a dune buggy. Dylan threw out another grenade. The grenade landed in front of the Demon. This time the blast blew him back several feet.

There were two giant dogs that ran beside the dune buggy. When the grenade exploded, the two dogs leaped onto the creature's wings and instantly ripped them off. Then each of the dogs bit the general by his arms and held him in a crucified position.

Dylan held up a book in front of himself. He read some mystical sounding words from the book. A ball of fire shot out from the book and went right through the creature's chest. The beast fell backwards bending his knees at the joints.

As the beast fell, a crackling sound came from his legs. It was the sound of his bones breaking. He yelled…

"You'll never make it past my brother in the mountains."

"Let's go!" yelled Dylan. Jon ran to the dune buggy and jumped in.

"Thanks" Jon said in a casual manner.

As the General lay in the red sand facing up, he spoke his last words about Jon.

"Fool, you should have taken the deal! We still have what you desire most of all!"

The creature disintegrated into ash and blew away with the wind.

27

Dylan, Jon and the old lady drove away as fast as they could. The dune buggy was made to handle the roads of hell. The steering wheel was in the center of the vehicle and it had an excellent suspension system. On the back of the dune buggy was a bumper sticker that read "Made in U.S.A."

Dylan and Jon both looked at the old lady and were amazed of how strong she seemed. They did not know anything about her other then she was one tough woman.

The old lady yelled to them,

"We have to get to another one of Hell's Earths quickly! We must go to one that the Devil doesn't know about yet!"
They were going so fast that it was hard to hear her. The wind was blowing in their ears.
"I have a place in mind but we have to hurry and make sure that we are not being followed." She said.
The old lady brought the dune buggy to an abrupt stop. Jon and Dylan slammed against the front of the dune buggy.
"Now, everyone put their hands on the book!" She demanded.
After Jon and Dylan joined her hand on the book she chanted some magical words. A clear orb of energy formed around them.
The old lady continued,
"Good. That should keep us safe from him finding us. Let's go! The dogs will take care of anything that tried to follow us."
As they drove away they could see the two dogs behind them in the distance. It appeared that one of the dogs had caught a demon bird that was trying to follow them.

141

The dog locked his jaws onto the possessed bird's neck, killing it instantly.

The old lady continued,

"You're going to need this safe haven in order to learn the powers of the book. The powers you will need for your journey. It's destined."

"There are a lot of them, you know? And he can be any one of them."

"What do you mean?" asked Dylan. Jon also listened the best he could, despite how fast they were going.

She answered,

"Like I said before, this is his land. This is his realm and his soldiers. He has his generals and then his army. And they have been busy lately. He'll send his generals out to look for you. Then, when one of them finds you, he will be able to see you through their eyes. He has the power to turn into them. Not at full strength"

The old lady became excited with warning, "He will hunt you! He will never stop! He will kill you! He will kill everything in his path that tries to stop him. He is the Devil. And we are on his playground!"

Dylan and Jon were speechless.

"Thanks a hell of a lot!" Jon replied sarcastically. "It was very inspirational. Now I'm inspired to die"

Jon and Dylan sat back in their seats. The old lady headed out an open road and drove towards the far hills. The giant dogs followed along side of them.

The land passed by fast. The lands red sand and hills were flashing in front of Jon's eyes. He was still high from the drugs he had done earlier. It gave him a calm numbness.

It was getting dark. The sky was red but darkness still set upon the land. It was nothing like Jon and Dylan had ever seen before. The land was made for death and destruction yet had a morbid kind of beauty.

The wind blew the sand all over the roads. Most of the time they were driving they had to make their own road. Luckily, the old lady knew how to navigate. They had to go just far enough to through off any of the Devils' trackers. They tracked their prey by scent. Once they reach one of Hell's Earths, they will be safe and they can get some rest.

There were many thoughts and unanswered questions that ran through Dylan's mind. But there was one questioned that needed to be answered right away. Dylan asked the old lady politely, "What is your name?"

"Meredith," she answered.

Dylan thought of an aunt named Meredith that he once had. She was his father's sister. Dylan never knew her. He was a baby when she died. His father never liked to talk about her.

Over a tall sandy hill, they drove up to one of Hell's Earths. They saw the outlines of trees and plant life. But once they crossed over onto the Earth's side it automatically turned into day. It was a relief just to see plant life again.

"This is one of the very few lands of Earth in Hell. Not too many know about this land. It was blessed by a living human. God had granted him the power. That usually never happens. "

At the end of the long grassy road was an old farmhouse. It had a wooden porch with a swinging bench.

"It's not much to look at, but it will do for now," said Meredith.

Behind the house there was a big barn. There were some animals grazing in the background. The farm had chickens, ducks, pigs, cows and the two dogs.

The big white German Sheppard was named Petey and the black Pit Bull was named Rocky. They were the ones who kept the farm animals in order. They were also very intelligent. They related with all different life forms even humans.

They pulled up in front of the house. Jon and Meredith started to walk up the porch. Meredith turned to Dylan and said, "No, not you boy, you and that book of yours have to go around back to the barn. It's reinforced with different spells and holy things for protection. You can't just be throwing spells all r extra pro around and not expect someone to notice." Meredith said to Dylan. She took a look at Dylan and seen how dirty he was. Meredith realized how aggressive she has been. She has not had any pleasant company in a long time.

Meredith calmly responded,
"You can come in the house to clean up and such. I'll fix you all up some food. I'll come get you when it's ready."

 Meredith then quickly turned to look at Dylan face to face. Dylan was a little intimidated by the big round goggles she whore on her face.

"Oh and Dylan, never let that book out of your sight. Never let anyone hold it. Never let anyone read it. And trust no one. Not even us."

28

Jon and Dylan sat in the living room while Meredith served them some food. Jon gazed into the memory of his last fix. He thought about the dope he had from the cowboy dealer in the ally. Jon reminisced the powerful feeling it gave him. It gave him the feeling of tremendous strength and courage. He feared nothing!

"Snap out of it!" Meredith smacked Jon on the back of his head to break his daydream. "Weak minded you are!"

Meredith unrolled a map onto the table.

"To you, it is the Atlantic Ocean," Meredith began to tell Jon and Dylan about their journey tomorrow.

"Down here it is just a flat desert land. The dune buggy will sail nicely. It will run like lightning on the special fuel. It will give you a maximum speed of 250 miles per hour. But make sure you have open land. Crashes on the dune buggy are nasty! But they're strong. You are not. Just roll with it! On a flat surface you will make good time." Meredith showed them where the flat surfaces were on the map.

"You should get some rest Jon. You are going to have to focus. If any of the generals find you you're going to need your strength," said Meredith.

"How am I going to protect us from the generals of the Devil?" asked Jon sarcastically.

"More shall be revealed. On his time Jon, not yours. You are stronger then you think. I hope, anyway." Meredith replied then turned her attention to Dylan.

"Dylan, you go into the barn tonight and study that book. Don't worry about sleeping. You can sleep tomorrow when you are on the road."

"You're not coming with us?" asked Dylan.

Meredith answered,
"No. I can't Dylan. After you leave tomorrow my services will no longer be required. I will be no more. My service here will be fulfilled and I hope to be set free."
Dylan then replied passionately,
"Then, tomorrow, when we separate, I shall be happy for you!" Dylan gave her a hug and thanked her.

"You are wise, Dylan. You have the wisdom that is greater than many kings" she said.

29

Flashes of light and weird sounds came from the barn that night. The barn doors were closed but light seeped through the cracks in the wooden walls.

Dylan opened one of the barn doors and came running out. He ran up to the porch where Meredith was sitting.

"Do you have any holy water?" Dylan asked as he panted for air.

"Yes. I have some holy water." She responded in a soft tone. She was not surprised at all by what was going on in the barn or by his question.

"All the water on this land is holy. It has all been blessed." Meredith said.

"Something wrong Meredith?" Dylan asked.

150

Meredith looked nothing like the beast she was when he first saw her. Her skin tone was now that of a younger woman. Dylan could still tell she was sad.

"This has been my home for a long time. I believe I will miss it, even if it is Hell." Meredith responded and then took a deep breath. Even though most of her beastly features had faded away, she still wore her goggles. She had worn those goggles the whole time and not once taken them off. She continued,

"But, just like anywhere in the universe, my home and inner peace come from inside. No matter where I go, I always take myself with me, in this life and the next. And the ones that follow. The rules are the same no matter when you live. For every one of something good, there is an equal opposite of bad. Love has hate. Sadness has joy. These are all universal feelings."

"People, birds, rabbits, and fish all have the same feelings. Even the plant life can feel. We once lived as all of those things, you know? It's where we came from." Meredith shared her knowledge with Dylan.

"Everything in Hells Earth is blessed. You will find some weapons behind the black cover in the barn. All of the arrows and bullets are made from this land. Even the swords' blades are made from the metal from this land."

"Who are you really?" asked Dylan.

Meredith felt uncomfortable about the question. She did not answer right away. She had made some tea and poured them each a cup.

Then she went over to a treasure chest that she had in the corner. Out of it came another map. This map was different than the other maps. It was on very fragile paper. The paper was so brittle that you could see through it.

"This will show you how to get to the Holy land you seek. It will also show you the other places from earths that are blessed lands here. You can use these places if you need to rest or take cover. They are all different in ways. But they all have supplies and weapons to defeat the damned."

Meredith carefully handed Dylan the map. "Put the map in the book and the book will lead you.

The map paper is frail. That is so the damned won't get it. The paper will burn up instantly when any one of the damned touches it."

Dylan put the map into the book and it magically absorbed into the pages.

Meredith finally answered Dylan's question.

"I was a sister to your father." She said. "Once I was human just like you. I did something stupid and ended up here in hell. I was destined to live in hell and serve the Devil for all eternity. But, thanks to you, I have a chance to redeem myself. I have a chance to be forgiven. And tomorrow, when you leave out of here alive, I will be set free!"

Meredith was holding something back. Dylan could tell that she was not telling him everything.

"You must go and finish reading the book. Petey and Rocky will rotate standing guard at the border of Hells Earth and they will keep you company tonight. They can speak our language as long as they are on holy ground. So, don't be startled if one of them starts to talk to you."

Dylan thanked Meredith for the tea and headed back to the barn.

30

Jon awoke and sat up in bed. He was soaked with sweat. He was in the bedroom of the farmhouse where Meredith had taken him and Dylan.

"Shit! I was hoping I was just dreaming", Jon said to himself about being in Hell.

Unknown to Jon, he was in trouble. There was a giant black snake with red glowing eyes slithering around his room. Jon was still dreaming.

A noise came from the far corner of the room. It sounded like something had got knocked over.

"Who's there?" Jon asked in fear.

There was no answer. Jon looked around the room. There was a hissing sound coming from one side of the room. As Jon stared into the dark corner another hissing sound came from the other side of the room. Jon froze. He became so scared that he was paralyzed with fear. He could not move. He could not speak.

Out of the dark corner of the room leaped a red-eyed snake toward Jon. The snake had its mouth wide opened. Jon could see its long fangs and pointed tongue coming towards him.

Right before the snake was able to bite Jon, another snake leaped from the other side of the room and tackled the red-eyed snake to the floor.

The two snakes tangled themselves together and started fighting. The second snake looked the same as the red-eyed snake except it had white leathery skin and blue eyes.

Jon could not tell if he was dreaming or if this was real. Jon swung his legs over the edge of the bed and stood up. Jon felt something slimy wrap around his leg. It was the tail of the red-eyed snake. The red-eyed snake's tail had wrapped around the room, under the bed and around Jon's leg. Jon became frozen with fear again as the tail pulled his feet out from under him. Jon's face hit the floor. Without the white snake knowing, the black snake wrapped his tail

156

around Jon's neck and proceeded to choke him.

After a short battle, the white snake sank his fangs into the black snake's neck. The black snake began to die and he loosened his grip on Jon. Jon quickly stood up and ran out of the room.

When Jon ran out of the bedroom, he ran into the living room. Only it wasn't the farmhouse living room. It was the living room of his old house. The house he and Michele, his wife, used to live before their tragedy.

Jon took a look around. He had noticed that the door to the basement was opened. Jon walked over to the door and went down the stairs into the basement.

When he got to the bottom of the stairs, he saw that nobody was there.

Jon walked over to an old couch. Jon use to get high on this couch before he got evicted.

Jon sat down on the couch. He looked down at his hands and saw he was holding two bags of heroin. They both had a red stamp called "DEVIL". Jon glanced at the other end of the couch and saw a needle

157

lying on the cushion with everything he needed to work up a fix.

"This is too good to be true!" Jon said to himself. He mixed up the heroin.

Jon held up the needle and tapped out the air bubbles. In the background, a little girl had appeared. Watching what Jon was doing.

Jon was confused. But he still wanted to do his hit of heroin. He rolled up his sleeve and inserted the needlepoint into his vein. He drew back on the plunger and his blood gushed into the needle, mixing with the heroin. Just before Jon could push in the plunger, the little girl quickly walked up to him, pulled the needle out of his arm, and stabbed him right in the eye with the needle!

Jon sat up in his bed holding his eye in a panic. He felt around his face to make sure everything was okay. His clothes and sheets were completely wet from sweat. He took a moment to gather his thoughts. He felt a sharp pain in his stomach. Jon heard a lot of commotion going on outside.

"They're here! Time to go! They're here!" yelled Meredith.

158

"They're here!" yelled Meredith as she broke open the barn doors. Dylan had his head down inside the book on the table. He must have fallen asleep through the night.

The dune bug was all ready loaded with the supplies that they were going to need on their journey. Food, water, fuel and anything holy enough to stake a demon, were all stowed away on the dune buggy. Most demons disintegrate when something holy breaks their skin. The bigger demons and their generals take a lot more to be destroyed. Everything from Hell's earth is holy.

Jon came out of the house and stumbled down the steps. He was in bad shape. The drugs that he did yesterday were more potent than anything he has ever done. As every addict knows, the higher you get, the harder you fall. He had to detoxify off of heroin before, but nothing like this. Jon looked like he had his life sucked out of him.

Dylan and Meredith both stood there looking at Jon as he helped himself off the ground.

"I'm okay," said Jon. Then he bent over and threw up.

"Is this guy supposed to protect me or am I supposed to protect him?" Dylan asked sarcastically.

Meredith finished fastening the cargo.

"Do you have the book?" she asked.

"Right here," Dylan said showing his satchel.

"Remember; don't ever let it out of your sight. The Devil has the greatest sneaks and snakes that ever lived. Also, he himself is powerful. All of the land outside of Hell's Earth is his house. He can alter what you see, what you hear and for some, he can control what you think and feel. When he turns into another life form, he does not have all his powers right away. The spells I put on you should hide your location so he won't know where you are. Unless you give them permission and break the spell."

  Meredith gave a rundown of everything that they needed to know. She pointed her finger onto Dylan's chest and said,

"Trust no one. Not even those closest to you. Maybe that's why God has chosen Jon as a Guardian; he is just as sneaky and slimy as

160

the rest of the snakes. It takes a snake to know a snake!"

"What's with all the snakes?" asked Jon before fainting.

  Jon thought of his dream as he laid there blacked out. Did it have any prevalence? If so, what did it mean? Maybe it meant nothing. Jon couldn't think straight. His mind was racing with thoughts of human insanities. In a way, he was hoping that this was all a dream and he would wake up soon. And he did. Meredith threw a bucket of water on Jon to revive him. Jon got up and they all loaded into the dune buggy.

31

The dogs barked loudly at the border of Hell's Earth. The grass road turned into red sand at the border. Rocky had just returned to join Petey. He had gone to alert Meredith of the trackers arrival. There were only two demon dogs on Hell's side. The demon dogs had a solid black color with glowing red eyes. All of the creatures of the dammed have glowing red eyes. Each of the damned dogs had a spiked collar. Skulls, bones and blood from their previous kills dripped off their spikes and fangs.

All of the dogs barked and growled at each other, but neither would dare cross the borderline. Once they have crossed onto the other side of the land they will forfeit any special abilities that they possess and they will be at the mercy of their enemies.

This was not the first time Petey has met one of these dogs. He wasn't afraid, but he knew that if he were to cross over to hell's side he would surely be at a disadvantage.

One of the damned dogs stopped barking and ran into a pathway of hell. The walls of the pathway were similar to the walls of a canyon.

He was, with no doubt, going to alert the generals of their location. The demon dogs were not certain about Jon and Dylan being there, but they knew that the good dogs were there and they traveled with the old woman.

With a good chance of the book being there, the devil himself will surly appear with his army. If that happens, the boy and his guardian will never get out of there alive.

Petey stooped his head down and then leaped over the boundaries into hell. He began to chase the demon dog. Rocky pleaded for Petey not to leave and to return back to the blessed land. But Petey didn't listen. He couldn't listen because he lost the ability to communicate when he crossed over the boundaries. Petey ran down the trail and disappeared behind the rocks.

"It's a trap!" yelled Rocky. But it was too late.

As soon as Rocky finished those words, the other damned dog stopped barking and smiled at Rocky. His smile was deceitful and scary. The demon dog turned around and began to take chase to Petey.

"No. No. No. Why? Why? Why?" Rocky said to himself over and over again while he paced back and forth. Rocky did not have as much courage as Petey. Rocky was brave but he always had Petey by his side. Now, Petey was not by his side nor was he by Petey's side. Now, just as a human would struggle with such emotions, Rocky must look inside himself to find the courage to save his friend.

Finally, Rocky said, "What the hell?" and took a leap out of Hell's Earth and into the land of the damned. Rocky gave chase to the demon dogs down the red rocked trail.

32

Meredith, Jon, and Dylan made it to the end of a long grassy road. It was the end of Hells Earth and the beginning of Hell. They were on the backside of the land.

"This is it!" said Meredith. "This is as far as I go with you! We don't have time for a long good bye. They will soon have the entire land surrounded with the Damned Army. Nothing will be able to leave. So, now go! Good luck and God speed!" said Meredith.

"One thing I must know Meredith. Or should I say Aunt Meredith?" Dylan asked her.

"Yes, Dylan, I am your father's sister. I am your aunt. I am ashamed for what I have done. But thanks to you." Meredith stopped and almost started to cry. "No one ever…" she became choked up again and had to stop talking. It took a lot for her to get out those couple of words.

Jon and Dylan were amazed at how this woman transformed over night. She transformed from a beastly creature into a beautiful woman. She did it with strength and courage against some of the most fearful creatures that have ever lived. And here she was, getting all choked up just saying good-bye.

"Go now and remember what I have told you."

Jon took over driving the dune buggy and Dylan strapped himself in to a seat in the back. Jon looked over at Meredith and gave her a nod goodbye. He revved up the engine, dropped the clutch into gear and launched across the boundaries into Hell.

33

Petey caught up to the demon dog. He jumped on his back and dragged him to the ground.

"Foolish dog, you can't even understand me unless I let you. Your life is now over!" said the Demon dog as he leaped into the air and knocked Petey to the 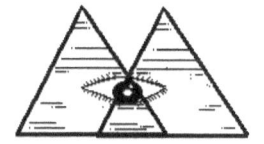 ground. He snapped his sharp teeth to get Petey by the neck. Luckily, Petey moved out of the way just in time. The fight was vicious to the end.

The two dogs snapped and bit each other hoping to clamp on tight enough to get the final kill. There was blood all over everything. It was all over their fur and dripping from their teeth. The demon dog threw Petey up against a big rock. When Petey bounced off of the rock he left a bloodstained outline of his body. Petey lay there panting heavy against the rock.

"You are foolish for thinking you could defeat me," said the demon dog.

"You're the fool", said Petey as he panted out of breath. "I didn't need to defeat you; I just needed to slow you down!"

The demon dog paced for a moment.

"So, they are here!" said the demon dog surprisingly.

A voice shouted behind them,

"And he isn't coming out until he is ready to kick all of you out of Hell!" It was Rocky.

"And he's going to have one less ass to kick when I'm done with you." Rocky strolled out from behind the rocks. He had his head held high and ready to battle.

"You don't stand a chance, not in my Hell!" said the demon dog.

34

Jon was traveling at a good speed. The land was flat and bare. The only wind was from the speed of the buggy. They both wore goggles to keep the sand out of their eyes.

After they were a few miles away, they took a look back at Hell's Earth. They could see blue skies with beams of sunlight shooting out from behind white clouds. It was  a beautiful horizon that stretched from as far as you could see.

A huge dust cloud rose from the south of Hell's Earth and another formed from the north. It was the Army of the Damned. Ordered to surround that piece of Hell's Earth and kill all that tried to enter or leave.

Jon wanted to get as far away as possible. About twenty minutes later, something happened that struck fear into their hearts.

They looked back at Hell's Earth. The skies above Hell's Earth had been engulfed in red. The beautiful colors of Hell's Earth had been shadowed in with darkness and the skies were gelled red. The Devils Army had completely surrounded the grounds. Nothing was going to get out. Not alive. An evil presence lurked on the horizon. Jon and Dylan had a feeling that he, the Devil himself, had arrived.

35

Rocky was dog fighting with the demon
dog. He sunk his tooth into the demon dogs
left eye. His tooth broke off inside the
demon dog's eye. It made it hard for the
demon dog to see. Rocky was wearing
him down. With every leap he took a little
piece of the demon dog with him.
"This is such a waste of time. My partner is
well on his way to tell the generals our
location," said the demon dog.
"Well, I guess he won't be needing this."
said Rocky as he tucked his head behind a
boulder and dragged out the spiked leash
from the other demon dog.
Rocky dropped the leash on the ground and
walked over to Petey.

Petey was lying in a pool of his own blood.
Rocky stood over top of Petey. Rocky took
one look at Petey and knew that he didn't
have much time left to live. Petey's white fur
was saturated with blood. It was at that
moment when Rocky and Petey truly
understood how precious time really was.
"He is laying on the ground about 50 yards
back down the trail. If you're lucky, maybe
you can go bleed to death with him!" said
Rocky to the demon dog.
"Not without your blood to fill our thirst!"
the demon said as he leaped into the air. He
snapped his jaws into Rocky's neck. He
latched down hard on his throat and took
him down. Just as they landed onto the
ground, Petey sat up and sank his teeth
right into the neck of the demon dog. Petey's
jaws clamped down on the dogs neck so
hard that he crushed the demon dog's
throat. The demon dog slowly let go of
Rocky's neck.
  Rocky ran over to the spiked collar and
grasped it in his mouth. Petey knew that this
was the moment he was here for. Petey used
all his strength to hold the demon dog down
on the ground. Rocky leaped into the air

and landed on top of the demon dog, driving the spikes through the demon dog's chest, neck, and head. The demon dog's mouth was wide open, when a spike emerged out from the back of his throat. Not a sound came out of the demon dog. He slowly fell over. He was dead.

"We did it!" Rocky tried to say but only barks came out. He could not communicate with Petey. Petey lied there panting very slowly. Rocky wanted to say so much to him but only barks came out when he tried. Rocky looked deep into Petey's eyes and hoped that he could read everything he wanted to say.

Rocky figured it's probably better off not being able to speak because he would not know how to tell him that the other demon dog had got away. He managed to slow him down and rip off his collar but he lost him on the chase.

Rocky started to nudge Petey as if it was time to leave. But Petey was not moving. Petey knew back when he took that leap into hell that it was going to be a one-way trip for him. Petey looked at Rocky. He gave him a blink and a smile. Then he fell into a blank stare. It looked like he was staring at the most wonderful thing that he had ever seen. Petey took his last breath and then passed away.

Rocky bowed down to Petey in honor. Tears ran down Rocky's eyes. He had so much to say but all he could do was howl. He howled the songs that they used to sing with Meredith at the barn house while they waited for the boy and his guardian. He thought Petey would like that.

Petey lay in the red desert sand. Rocky was waiting for Petey's body to turn and vanish out of existence.

Suddenly, a heavenly glow shined off of Petey. Petey started to turn to dust. His dust particles had a golden glow. The golden particles floated away into the sky. Petey's destiny had been fulfilled.

As Rocky watched the golden particles vanish into the sky, he noticed a row of demon dogs had lined up on the boulder tops. Another line of demon dogs had lined up on the other side of the boulder tops. Rocky was surrounded.

36

Rocky noticed a demon dog with his collar missing. He was the same demon dog that Rocky had chased earlier. The demon dog approached with a general.

The general addressed Rocky, "I'm glad to see you still have my pet's collar. I am also glad to see that you have taken your last breath! Kill him!" he ordered.

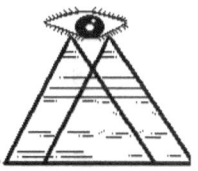

Suddenly, there was an explosion right in front of the demon dogs.

37

Meredith stood on top of a boulder with a grenade in her hand.

"You will not touch my dog!" Meredith demanded.

Everyone stood still.

"Foolish woman, you leave yourself wide open for an easy kill out here," said the general.

"Go ahead, I want you to try, puppy dog." The demon general leaped into the air towards Meredith. His fangs hung out of his mouth, dripping with saliva, ready to rip into Meredith. Suddenly, something from the sky smashed the demon dog to the ground! A dust cloud emerged and blocked everyone's view.

A deep, dark voice spoke out,

"No, you fool!"

It was the Devil!

It was the Devil himself! He had taken the form of a high general. He had some powers and was slowly transforming into a bigger creature. He had enough power to handle Rocky and Meredith. He quickly turned to Meredith and snapped his fingers all but once. A medieval wooden body lock instantly locked onto Meredith. It wrapped around her mid section and locked her hands in place by her side.

"Don't drop your grenade," said the Devil.

The Devil then turned to Rocky and pointed his finger at him. A beam of electricity blasted off of his finger and made ankle shackles for all four of Rocky's legs. He even made a ball and chain for Rocky's tail.

"Ahahaha!" laughed the Devil.

Meredith screamed as she jumped off the boulder to attack the Devil. But the Devil was too fast. He turned and caught Meredith in the air with his magical powers.

"Go ahead. Do it! Do it! Kill me! Go ahead!" antagonized Meredith to the Devil.

"What? Don't you have any balls demon man? Or should I say demon boy? Go ahead! Do it! Kill me demon! Kill me!" Meredith pleaded.

"No!" The Devil shook his head no and began to chuckle.

"I will not help you fulfill your destiny. I will not send you to the place you should have already gone. You will pay the consequences for your sacrifice. You sacrificed your own destiny to save this pathetic dog. Oh, no! In fact, I am going to make sure that you never die and I am going to make sure your eternal life is nothing but torture and pain. I am going to make sure that you will never reach your destiny. The destiny you so poorly sacrificed. Your reconciliation was fulfilled until you stepped onto my soil. You should have stayed on Hell's Earth. As long as you stay alive on my soil the gates of Heaven will not open for you. You will have no way out. Unless…" He paused and started with his demented laugh again.

"You know of the other way out. And you know where that will take you. You are nothing. You will always be nothing. You are my slave and you will bow before me. Now!" demanded the Devil, "and forever you shall remain my slaves!"

  Meredith and Rocky were forced to their knees by the demon dogs. Meredith and Rocky were both thinking the same thing. They both knew it was not going to end good for them. At least the boy got away safe.

JON'S SECOND DREAM

Jon awoke from his dream or so he thought. He was in a panic. His head and body were pouring out sweat. He gasped for air and then started breathing heavy. He took a look around the room but did not recognize anything and he did not see anybody. He was squeezing his hands to make a fist. His fingers felt numb and tingled. His arms were bothering him. It felt as if there was something inside his veins. It was traveling up and down inside his arms, looking for a way out.
"Maybe it's looking for the hole where I stuck the needle", Jon thought. Jon took a look down at his arms and saw he had several holes up and down his arms. Each hole was the size of a penny and ran along

his vein lines. They were swollen and infected. The holes swelled in and out as if they were breathing.

Jon could see a black substance traveling along his veins. Jon was starting to get panicky. He started shaking his arms profusely. There was a ringing in his ears. Then, the ringing turned into voices. Angel voices. They were calling out his name. Jon stumbled outside the cabin house and slammed onto the dirt ground.

They had reached this little part of Hell's Earth after nightfall. Dylan stayed awake for most of the first half of the trip. Then he slept the rest of the way in. Jon managed to carry Dylan into the house and lay him on the sofa when they arrived. That was about the only thing he did before falling asleep in the bedroom. As Jon slept this is what he had dreamed.

"What the fuck did I do?" Jon yelled at himself.

"Why didn't that shit just kill me? So I can be fucking tortured?" Jon was being sarcastic with himself.

"The higher you go the harder you fall. What do you want from me? What do you want?" Jon pleaded as he began to act crazy.

The angel voices had suddenly stopped calling his name. Everything stood still and fell silent. Jon could not even hear his own breathing. And then a voice echoed through Jon's head.

"You know what I want?" Jon knew the voice. It was the voice of the deceiver. He was the same deceiver that sold him that last batch of heroin.

"All we want is the boy." The voice whispered. A dream cloud formed above Jon. In the dream cloud, Dylan was sleeping on the sofa.

"No." Jon whimpered like a beaten man.

Jon thought to himself, why the boy and not just the book.

The image then turned into money, and a mansion, and other luxuries of a wealthy person in Jon's lifetime.

"Everything you ever dreamed!" whispered the deceiver.

The image then swirled into a needle and a pile heroin.

"And, I have an instant cure for your pain,"
Said the deceiver in an almost pleasant tone.
  Jon replied, "The higher you go, the
harder you fall."
  Jon started to see flashing in his mind.
They were not the flashes like the heroin
high he had earlier from the deceiver. These
flashes were different. It reminded Jon of
the dream he had when he was climbing the
huge white pillars. Every stroke he took
with his wings and every leap he took with
his legs flashed through his mind. It
reminded him how fast and how strong he
could be.
"The strength I had. The strength it took to
move those wings," thought Jon to himself.
"It seemed so easy. My wings he thought. I
am strong. I can be strong."
"I must break Free!" Jon cried out loud and
stretched out his arms. Jon exploded with
strength. He pumped out his chest and every
muscle in his body. Jon was strong and Jon
wanted to break free!
  **The dream cloud dissipated and blew away
through the trees. Jon franticly woke up.
Everything went back to normal. Jon had
settled down and looked over his shoulder.**

182

Dylan was standing there. Dylan had seen everything that had just happened. Dylan gave Jon a nod of approval as his trust for Jon had grown. Dylan turned and walked back into the house.

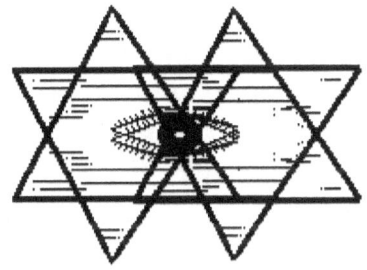

39

"Where are they, witch!" the Devil demanded and then slapped Meredith across her face. Not even a face as beautiful as hers could calm the Devil's anger. One of Meredith's goggle lenses had cracked. She had bruises on her face and her lip started to bleed.

"Why have they not come out looking for you? Do they not care about you? No. Wait." The Devil walked around and looked at the surroundings of Hell's Earth. He looked to the left. He looked to the right. Then he paced around and came to a sudden stop. Meredith took one look at the Devil and knew that the gig was up. All hell was about to break loose.

"They are not here!" yelled the Devil.

Then, something happened that no one ever lived to tell. The Devil became enraged. It was not a rage of normal anger. Murder, theft, failure, even betrayal are ways of justifying anger, that could be understood. All of the Damned Army had seen the Devil get angry before. Not like this. This anger came from humiliation. He had been tricked. They had made him look like a fool on his own land, in his own house. The Devil had been embarrassed in Hell.

The Devil raised his hands and he began to grow to a tremendous height. His arms turned into huge, black whips that he used to pummel down on top of his own soldiers and generals. Then with one sweep of his arms he crushed everything on this side of Hell's Earth.

There were a couple of his soldiers that had survived his sweep. They were crawling on the ground and could barley move. The Devil had raised his arms again and they formed into pointed spikes. They began to spawn off like roots growing from a tree. The spikes plunged into each of the remaining soldiers' bodies and ripped them in half.

Finally, his arms turned into huge twisters. They sucked up the remaining soldiers that were surrounding the other side of Hells

185

Earth. They too died in such a gory manner. The only remaining creatures were stumbling around slowly dying or burning. The Devil had killed them all. Hell never looked so morbid. This day was pronounced the day of "Hell's Massacre". The day was named in the book Dylan was carrying.

186

40

Meredith and Rocky gazed across the blood stained land that surrounded Hell's Earth. They could have never imagined that so much more destruction could be done to a place that was already destroyed. The remainder of the Devil's army was being burned. They were all in flames. Some were running around aimlessly.

Others just lay there dead or dying. The demon dogs tried to run and put themselves out, but they were too badly burnt. They fell over and burned into ash.

Anything in the desert land that could burn did burn. Meredith and Rocky actually felt sorry for them.

A large ring of fire surrounded Meredith and Rocky. The flames were more than ten foot high.

Out from the flames he walked. At first, you could only see his shadow. The shadow was getting larger. He was getting stronger and more powerful. He strutted out of the flames full pride for what he had just done. He walked alone and satisfied. His appearance alone was strikingly fearful. His legs and mid section were of an ox. They bared the color of the blackest oil. His body was the shape of human but gigantic in size. He was very red and very muscular. His head had a set of black horns that were bigger than any rhino. They had a glossy shine and pointed tips. In all he appeared as a red giant. The Devil was almost at full power now. This was just one of his many forms.

  The killings of his own kind seemed to fulfill his anger. Just like a wild animal, his hunger and thirst still ran rapid.

"This is what I can do! And soon, all of Heaven and Earth will see the same fate!" said the Devil as he held his arms up to point out his destructive creations.

The Devil raised his arms above his head. The land around them began to twist and spin.

  When everything stopped spinning, Meredith and Rocky were in the Devil's palace. They were chained to a stoned wall and new guard dogs were in place. In the middle of a huge room was a circular pool of darkness. The water was twirling around. A red fog floated everywhere. There was no floor yet you were still able to stand and walk. When Meredith took a hard look inside the water she could see an image of the boy and the Guardian. Then an image of Meredith appeared in the dark water. She walked over to the boy.

"Meredith" a voice whispered softly. "You know what we want." The voice was deceiving.

In the dark water the image of Meredith took out a knife and cut Dylan's throat. When the image turned towards the real Meredith the image showed her with glowing red eyes. Meredith had the eyes of the damned.

Meredith was having trouble with the images she was seeing. She did not want to be possessed and do the work of the Devil, not anymore.

"Not by my hands!" said Meredith. A demon dog had been walking past Meredith. She grabbed him with her legs and squeezed him back into her. The spikes from the

189

demon dog's collar plunged into Meredith's body. Her blood ran out and she quickly died.

"Suicide again?" said the Devil.

   This was her only chance to fix what she had done on earth. And now, she did it again. This time there was no redemption.

   Meredith's lifeless body hung on the chains until she turned into red sand and blew away with the wind.

The Devil smiled. He was pleased with the outcome.

"When Meredith returns, she will still belong to me."

41

Jon and Dylan have been traveling all day and night. They crossed over what would be known as the Atlantic Ocean on Earth. In Dylan's lifetime it was filled with water and wild life. Now it is just a flat, dried out land. Jon let Dylan drive the dune buggy when  they reached the flattest land across the bottom of the ocean. Their journey was long and tiring.

Dylan often thought of his family and wondered if he would ever see them again. He missed his mother. He missed the way she held his hand at night until he fell asleep. He figured his dad would also be pretty proud of him right now. If he saw how he was doing the right thing, no matter the odds. Dylan worried about his sister the

191

most. Together, they felt a special connection. Together they felt complete. Now she was not with him. Now she was on her own, and so was he. Every time Dylan thought of his home it gave him the strength and courage to go on.

They took shelter at another one of Hell's Earths later that night. It was a small piece of land right before the coast. It was like an island in the sea of sand.

Most of the holy lands in hell were in the bible. On the map in the book, a triangle with a circle glowed gold, which revealed the lands that had become blessed.

Jon was feeling a lot better. The worst was over as far as having opiate withdraws. The abscesses on his arms were beginning to heal and Jon was getting the feeling back in his hands. His bones and joints ached but that was to be expected until he builds his strength.

The drug cravings and insomnia were going to be a battle. After some time, that too shall pass and the cravings will only be occasional, hopefully.

42

Jon and Dylan finally reached the beginning of the Ural Mountains. There were no blessed lands from Earth around here. From here on in there will be no shelter for them. There will be no place to hide. They have to make it all the way through the frozen forest without stopping. Just beyond the mountains lies the Holy Land. The Holy Land will give the book the power to open the right door to Dylan's world. Then they can go home. Dylan had been studying the book through the whole journey. He learned how to use the fireballs and create a halo force shield. There was a spell to throw off trackers and to protect their location. A lot of the book was too much for Dylan to understand at his age. He did not get

193

discouraged. He remembered what Meredith had told him about the book. The book will only let him know what he needs to know. Even if he does not understand it now, he will understand it later, when the time is right.

  Jon and Dylan followed a rocky path through the hills to the mountains. The path had ended and it started to get cold.

"Here is the only place in hell that the temperature is not boiling hot. It is the land below freezing." Dylan said to Jon. "I read it in the book. The temperature is going to drop below freezing and there are going to be blistering winds. It is going to get so cold that our blood in our bodies will freeze and we will become a frozen treat for whatever can live here."

"How are we going to survive through this?" asked Jon.

"We need to have a little faith, Jon. We need to have hope and a lot of courage if we stand a chance." said Dylan.

"Now I know what that snowball feels like. Not a chance in Hell." Jon said sarcastically.

"There is a story behind why it is so cold here. I'll have to tell you later. Right now,

194

we have to get this tarp cover over the dune bug." Dylan told Jon.

Dylan was glad to see Jon in good spirits. He seemed to be healthier and not so much in a fog.

Dylan was still not for sure how much he could trust Jon. He's not high now. Will he need to get high later? Will the Devil be able to possess his mind again if he's weak? These are some of the fears that Dylan was holding onto.

Dylan knew that fears could be dangerous. He thought about what he knew about fear. He remembered his father teaching him about fear. He remembered him saying,

"Fear can be a good thing. You see, son, everything must have an opposite." His father said, "The opposite of fear is courage and bravery. Only from fear can courage and bravery emerge. If you are lucky enough to find yourself in a confrontation with fear, stand up! Defeat it with its opposite. It is your time to shine. It will be a moment in time to show that you are courageous and brave. It will be your moment. Let the courage and bravery run

195

through you. If you ever have doubt, remember truth and honesty always prevails. When courage and bravery become the victor there will be glory. Don't let the chance for glory pass you by! And know that in the end, win or lose, you did the right thing. "

Jon and Dylan finished putting the cover on the dune bug and started driving into the snowy pathway. Dylan sat with the book close to his lap.

Snow fell from the sky and landed on top of the dead and decaying trees. Not one living animal. Not one living tree was in sight. It was dead silent. There was not even a dead animal.

Jon said, "This is what I would call the "dead of winter"

Both of them were shaking and chattering their teeth.

"Look!" said Jon. "Your book, it's glowing!"

Dylan looked down and seen the symbols on the book were glowing. Dylan wasted no time opening the book. He opened to a page that was in the center of the book and was glowing blue. Jon took a peek at the book,

but he could not understand any of the
words.

"You can read that?" Jon asked Dylan.

"I can hear them too," answered Dylan.

"Yes! And I got some good news." Dylan
replied.

Dylan repeated a magical chant that he
read from the book. The chant had a
musical tone. The glow of the page became
brighter with every note and the book began
to change colors.

Dylan and Jon could feel themselves
warming up. The book was
giving off a lot heat. The
inside of the dune bug was
nice and warm. Jon and Dylan
started to celebrate with chuckles of
laughter and a sigh of relief.

They were starting to form a special bond.
Neither of them knew what was going to
happen next. Neither knew if they were
going to live or die or if they would ever see
home again. All they really had was each
other. Even though they just met a short
while ago, they felt they have known each
other for years. They both had a feeling; if

they stuck together they would be all right. Together, they would make it home.

"So, what happened?" asked Dylan.

"What do you mean?" replied Jon.

"I figured something bad must have happened to you," said Dylan.

"Why would you think that?" asked Jon.

"I can see it. It's in your eyes. I call it "The eyes of the walking dead", Dylan answered. "When I look into some people's eyes, I can just tell."

Jon understood what Dylan was talking about. They were becoming more comfortable in each other's company.

Jon told Dylan what had happened to him. Jon was able to tell Dylan the tragedy of his life. Jon has not talked about it in years. And to Jon's recall, he has never talked about it to anyone on a personal level.

The dune bug stopped abruptly.

"What's going on?" asked Dylan.

"The snow is too high for us to get through," said Jon. "We don't have that much further to go," said Dylan.

"Hey, do you see that?" asked Jon "What is that? Is that what I hope it is?"

Jon rolled up the dune bugs cover and stepped out into the snow. The snow was past his knees. Jon continued to walk, lifting each leg up to his chest to get through the snow.

"Oh, I don't like this Jon. Maybe you shouldn't go?"

Dylan peaked at the map and saw a red skull near their location.

Dylan was yelling to Jon but Jon could not hear him with the whistling winds blowing past. Jon continued to trot his way through the snow. When Jon was close enough he could see it was an old log house. It looked like there was a light on inside. 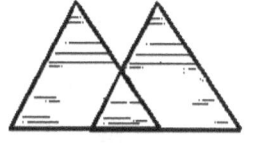 The smell of food roasting filled the air.

Dylan sat there for a moment. He closed his eyes to get a moment to relax. He thought of a cartoon he and his sister used to watch. The cartoon was about a trap, set in the woods, with food cooking.

As soon as Dylan closed his eyelids he opened them back up.

"STOP, IT'S A TRAP!" Dylan screamed, but it was too late. By the time Dylan realized that Jon was walking into a trap, a

199

pack of demon wolves ascended out from the black forests' scenery. They quickly surrounded Jon and slowly gathered in on him.

 All of the wolves had fur that was of the purest white in color with shades of gray. Their eyes glowed red like the rest of the demons and they had long fangs. The wolves of the damned were a very different type of demon. They work tremendously well with each other. They have a telepathic language that is unknown to all other creatures. Only they can transfer their thoughts to one another. Because of this special sense, they have their own spiritual connection with each other. They are the elite of the Devil's army.

43

The cabin in the woods collapsed inward and went up in flames. Jon froze as he watched the cabin burn. Finally he realized, "This house was set here just for us. It was a trap. They knew we would be looking for shelter out here. How could I've been so stupid?"

Dylan noticed a crow watching them from a dead tree limb. It had red damned eyes. The crow jumped off the dead tree branch and began to fly toward Dylan. It flew passed Dylan and looked at him right in the eyes before flying off through the woods.

Dylan knew it was only a matter of time before the Devil found out where they were located. Their only chance to make it was to get to the Holy Land now. That was the only place for them to be safe.

Dylan moved into the driver's spot. He reversed the dune bug back over its tracks and then drove it forward over a dead tree branch and fallen trees. Dylan drove the dune buggy right off the rooted end the huge tree. He landed right into the middle of the wolf pack and next to Jon.

"Get in!" yelled Dylan. Jon jumped into the dune bug. "Thanks. Now what are we going to do?" Dylan opened the book that was already glowing. Dylan lifted his hand through a hole in the ceiling. He chanted some magical words that echoed back from the book. A blue and white ball shot out of his arm and up high into the sky. The ball twirled in mid air for a moment and then flew away. It appeared to have no effect on anything.

"What in Hell was that?" asked Jon. Dylan replied franticly "I don't know. Okay."

Jon said sarcastically,

"Oh. That did a lot of good. It looked pretty too; do you have any more fireworks?"

The wolves started to move in closer to the dune bug.

"Hurry" yelled Jon.

Dylan lifted his hand once again but this time set his hand on the ceiling of the dune bug. He repeated the words that he saw in the book.

A sudden force surged out of the book, through Dylan's arm and around the body of the dune buggy.

A dome shaped shield had popped out of the dune buggy and formed around the vehicle. One of the wolves had tried to attack them from behind but was blocked by the shield and knocked the wolf back into the snow.

"Wow! Awesome! Look at that. The shield is melting the snow all around us. Let's go!" said Jon.

"You drive Jon," said Dylan sarcastically.

"Gee, thanks, mister," responded Jon sarcastically.

The snow melted instantly when it touched the dome shield. They drove through the snow filled forest. They made their own pathway. The wolves gave chase.

There was one wolf in particular that led the chase. His name was Dakota. He was a Demon Wolf like no other. He was the leader of the Devil's Army of the Mountains and he was the army's greatest warrior. He knew how important the book was to the Devil. He knew its power.

Dakota wanted the book. For what? The book was the ultimate weapon in any battle, in any universe. Even in the battles between Heaven and Hell the book was deadly. He knew the one to hold that book would be one of the most powerful beings in the universe.

44

Dylan was trying to read the book but he could not get it opened. It was not glowing and the papers on the side would not move, bend or fold. They were solid. There was no way the book would open. Dylan was huffing and puffing. He was trying to open the book. The book would not budge. Dylan was becoming angry.

"What's with this thing? It won't let me open it," said Dylan. "This never happened before."

"It's only going to give you what you need," said Jon.

"This shield is working well for now."

"Yea, but I was still able to read it. Something isn't right" said Dylan.

The book will not open to those eyes that the book does not want it to. Unknown to Jon and Dylan, they were being watched. Following them from high in the sky was the

Devil's spy. It was a vulture. It soared above all the other creatures and birds. It over looked everything with its glowing red eyes. The vulture had excellent vision.

The book was aware that with just a few words from the sacred book will turn any friend into an enemy and any peace into chaos. Dylan was still so young and so pure that he does not realize how powerful the book really is. If the book fell into the wrong hands it could be used to change the balance for evil.

The book's story can have one of two endings. It can end with the triumph of good. All things will be at peace. Or it can end with evil being the victor. All will burn.

All of this power is in Dylan's hands. Dylan is starting to realize the responsibility of holding the book.

#

Dakota chased them down with five other demon wolves. The wolves kept throwing their bodies into the shield of the dune bug. They would slow it down with every strike but not do any damage.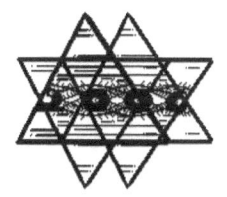

The path was getting rougher and it was getting harder to drive. There were dead and broken tree branches lying everywhere. Jon and Dylan still did not give up hope.

Dakota and two of his wolves managed to break ahead of Jon and Dylan. They found a tall tree down the path. They pushed the tree down to block the pathway. When Jon and Dylan approached the fallen tree, Jon tricked the dune buggy up onto two wheels

207

and launched off the roots of the tree. Now it was Jon and Dylan who were ahead.

   Finally, Jon and Dylan broke out of Hell's snowy forest. The dead trees and snow had ended and the red desert sand had begun again. The red desert sand stretched about ten miles to the beginning of the Holy Land. "We made it!" said Dylan excitingly as he was suddenly star struck by the wonder in front of him, the horizon of the Holy Land.

46

The Holy Land

The Pyramids of the Holy Land stood amazingly large. Even from a far distance their size was enormous. There were three main pyramids that towered over the city's buildings and temples. Jon and  Dylan were still too far away to see the city buildings just yet. Only the enormous pyramids stood as the horizon.

As they drove closer to the Pyramids their view of the city buildings became more visible.

The Pyramids did not appear old. They were made of golden sand, blocks of gold and pillars of diamonds that glittered from the rays of light that was shining from beyond the horizon. The background of blue

Hell's Earth copyright © 2015 by Pete Trolene
All Rights Reserved

skies enhanced the golden glow reflecting from the city. The view of the horizon gave off an uplifting feeling that magnified its beauty. Out of all the lands in the universe, this land was the most spectacular. This land was not like any other land. This land was the doorway to every planet ever made, at any time, in every dimension, in any lifetime. This land was not only holy but also powerful. This land is the land of God and this city is Heavens front door.

The Holy Land had many watchful eyes over looking its borders. Stationed along the wall surrounding the Holy Land stood tall pillars that had a pyramid shaped top. Inside the pyramid shaped top was a giant eyeball. The eyeballs levitated inside the pyramid and were able to look in any direction. They stood a careful watch. They are the Watchmen of the Holy Land and they have been waiting for this day.

One of the watchman's eyes spotted Jon and Dylan being chased across the final stretch of desert land. The eye blinked twice as it was assuring itself of what it was seeing. Then the whole pyramid-shaped top lifted off of the pillar and floated in the air to a round golden landing pad. When the eye landed on the circular pad an alarm sounded. A loud gong sound rang throughout the Holy Land. The sound was not like an ordinary gong. The sound was a pleasant heavenly tone. One note gave off a rhythm of sounds and echoes. This sound was a special sound. It was made for this exact moment in time. It was now time for the arrival of the bookkeeper and the return of the Holy Book.

 The gong rang through the Holy Land. The sound echoed through the streets and valleys of the Holy City. The streets were empty and no one was in sight.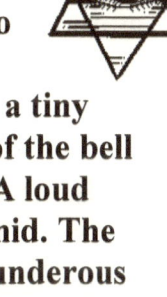

 At the base of the tallest Pyramid, a tiny crack started to form. Every gong of the bell made the crack split a little more. A loud rumble came from inside the Pyramid. The ground began to tremble. Loud, thunderous sounds came from inside the Pyramid that aided the cracking in the wall. Whatever was inside of this Pyramid was fearfully powerful and ready to break out.

The Devil finally received the message from the crow. The first spell that Dylan had shot into the air, back in the snowy forest, was not a waste after all. The blue and white ball had chased down and trapped the crow in a magical sphere. He could not relay an alert to the Devil of their presence in the mountains. The crow had to fly all the way to the Devil's castle to tell him of their location.

The Devil looked into the whirlpool of black souls. An image of Dylan and Jon appeared. They were being chased through hells desert to the Holy Land. The Devil instantly swirled around like a tornado and disappeared. He reappeared in front of his army of demons, inside the chambers of Hell. His army was awaiting his orders. They all had trained for this day. The day

the Devil uses his book to open a pathway
from Hell into Heaven.
"My children, it is time!" the Devil yelled
and all of the damned roared with him. The
damned army let out a thunderous roar
once more and charged into the darkness.

48

Jon and Dylan were way in front of the wolves. They have been traveling at top speed since the land flattened out.

The book had been glowing for a while. The book had been calling for Dylan to read it for a while. It was difficult for Dylan to read because the dune buggy was a rough ride at top speeds. Dylan tried to brace himself with one hand on the dune buggy's cross bar and the other hand holding the book. They hit a bump and the book popped out of Dylan's hand and the book closed, right when a spell was getting released. When Dylan was able to reopen the book, the book had lost its glow. Dylan was afraid he broke it.

"What the hell is that?" asked Jon.

Dylan thought Jon was talking about the book and answered,

"I don't know. It just lost its power. It closed on that last bump."

"No! Not that!" replied Jon. "Look! Over there!"

Far to the south, a mighty storm erupted.
All too much like the one they saw when
they left Meredith. The skies above the
sandstorm were wicked with black and gray
colors. Lightning bolts arched from cloud to
cloud. But what terrified them the most
were the lightning bolts that were lighting
up inside the sandstorm. Jon said to himself,
"It must be him! It must!"
Now, it was a race to the finish and the Holy
Land's front doors were the finish line.

The demon dogs, the generals on their chariots, and the rest of Hell's army joined the Mountain Wolves in the chase. The generals on the chariots whipped their pullers viciously. Their whips were made of chain links that had metal thorns sticking out of each link. With every lashing, the pullers flesh would be ripped from their bodies. The pain, however, enraged the beast. The beast used his rage for speed and would run extraordinarily fast. The wound on his flesh mended extremely quick and left a scar. The pullers back was completely mended with scars. Only to be reopened with the next whipping.

There were many advantages that the Devils army had on this land. It was the general's responsibility to use their powers to accomplish their mission.

One general noticed how difficult it was to travel up and down the sand dunes. The general carried a magical shank on the side of his belt. He took the shank in his hand and pointed it towards the horizon in front of him. A beam of light shot out of the shank and into the sky in front of them. Red, glittery sand crystals had fallen to the ground. The desert land of Hell mystically formed flat in front of the charging army. This allowed the Damned Army to reach top speed and gain on Jon and Dylan.

The soldiers carried weapons of slaughter and torture. Some of them carried sharp swords with jagged edges. Others carried ax type weapons. The giant goons carried a black jack (ball and chain with spikes).

In the rear of the army a convoy of cannons and catapults were being rolled in on logs. There was a series of movements that had to be done in order to move these huge weapons. The logs would be laid out with ten logs in front. Once a log was passed in the rear, a special breed of demons would lift the log and move it to the front of the row. It would take five demons to move one log. The process was repeated over and over. Because of the style of travel, the convoy moved much slower than the other soldiers.

These demons themselves, however, were very quick. They were slender with long skinny arms that they used to wrap around the logs. Despite their size and slenderness they were extremely strong.

In the skies above the Army of the Damned the condor birds added to the chase. The birds were not more than feathers and bone, but every bone on their wings could be used as a weapon. They would stake their prey with their wings and talons and pick them apart with their beak. Killing, to the birds, was natural.

The Army of the Damned had been training for this battle for centuries. They will fight to their death just to obey their master. They have no feelings or are they able to show mercy. This legion of demons had been specially bred, trained and equipped for this battle. This is the battle at Heaven's gate.

50

Dylan had asked himself, "How could the Holy Land of God have anything fearful? What could be holy enough to fight off the Army of the Damned?"

The dune bug was bouncing all over the place. Jon had the center wheel while Dylan was trying to send out a spell to help them.

"Hey, hurry up kid. I hope you can come up with something quick!" said Jon.

Dylan chanted some words and a bolt of energy shot out of the book, through Dylan's arm and hit the inside roof of the dune buggy. It knocked the cover off of the dune buggy and into the air.

"What the hell did that do?" Jon yelled in an upset tone.

"Well, at least you can see better!" answered Dylan.

The cover flew high in the air and was carried away by the wind. This left Jon and Dylan in plain view.

One of the Devil's chariots took lead of the chase. A general named Jackel controls the chariot. He began to catch up to Jon and Dylan. He whipped his puller viciously. The pullers were beasts born in a liter with the capability to heal their flesh. No sooner did the flesh heal from the chain whip another whipping would tear into the flesh of the puller.

The chariot now had a straight run to Jon and Dylan. In a matter of seconds Jackel will have them in his grasp.

Out of the sky above the general's chariot the cover from the dune buggy floated down and landed on top of the chariot's pullers. The pullers stumbled over their own feet and fell face first into the ground. The general and his chariot were thrown into the air and caused a big pile up for the army stampeding behind him. Two of the over sized goons, who were following close behind the chariots, were unable to stop and

they too stumbled over the fallen chariot.
When the big goons hit the ground they
bounced a few times and then began to roll.
They knocked over several other soldiers
and crushed those they rolled on. This
slowed down the lead chasers of the army.
But, soon after, another general took their
place and the chase continued.

The dune buggy lost its outer cover and the shield had worn away long ago. The only protection that they had was the roll bars on the dune buggy.

There were still some sand hills in Jon and Dylan's pathway. The army was quickly gaining on them.

"Hey kid, do you think that book has anything to help us out?" Jon asked and nodded to Dylan to look at the book. Dylan looked down at the book. It was glowing. "Oh shit!" Dylan had not recognized that the book had been glowing for some time. He immediately opened the book. This time Dylan didn't have to say or do anything. As soon as Dylan lifted the book cover, a golden blue ball of smoke shot into the air. When

222

the ball reached its peak in the sky it exploded like a firework. The explosion made golden dust particles that fell across the land in front of Dylan and Jon. As the gold dust landed on the ground it magically flattened the pathway. The road was clear. Jon and Dylan were amazed.

"Let's see what kind of special sauce Meredith made for this tin can, shall we?" Jon asked comically.

Jon looked down at the dashboard. There was a big red button that read "special sauce". Jon punched in the button. The dune buggy jolted, almost to a complete stall and then took off with miraculous speed. They quickly reached their top speed across the golden path.

"Underlay, Underlay! Arreaba!" Jon yelled out of the dune buggy. Dylan was plastered against the back of his seat.

He could feel the cheeks on his face being pulled towards the back of his head. Dylan put down the goggles that Meredith had given him earlier.

"That's so much better." said Dylan. His eyes were no longer being pushed up into his head. Dylan could finally see right. He looked at Jon and saw him catching bugs in his mouth.

Dylan stared at Jon as he drove them down the golden road. He watched as Jon's hair blew in the wind and his muscular body glistened from his sweat. Jon looked well and stood tall. Dylan thought for a moment. He thought maybe Jon could be a hero, a champion, or even a Guardian. For the first time, Dylan saw Jon in a positive way. For the first time in a long time, Jon saw himself in a positive way.255

Jon had regained his physical strength and his mind was clearing. It felt good to him to be released from the bondage of addiction. He had lost himself for many years and he forgot how it felt to be alive. He forgot how it was to feel. All the emotions that Jon had ever felt in his life, good or bad, had been numbed by the power he gave to his addiction. Jon forgot how it felt to be happy, to be joyful, and to love. Now, Jon can feel what it is like to be alive, again. Only this time he is in Hell. He is surrounded with nothing but negativity. Everything around him was made out of fear.

 Jon had been battling his demons this whole journey. He fought off his cravings every minute of every day. Jon denied temptation from the deceiver. He had been loyal to Dylan under great temptation. And now, he was fighting for something more than himself. He knew the importance of the book. He was aware of the consequences that would follow if Dylan and the book did not reach the Holy Land. Again, Jon had to ask himself, "Why Dylan and the book and not just the book?"

 Jon was on this journey on the sheer trust in hope. This is something that he had not done in a while. Jon had no hope nor did he trust anybody. Jon now had both. He had hoped they would make it to the Holy Land and he trusted in that hope.

 When Dylan first met Jon he did not trust him. Jon was arrogant and did not have any respect for life or for himself. To Dylan, Jon was a bum.

Even though Jon had no love for himself, there was still something special about him. Jon was not able to see any good in the world. His shine was dulled by his shameful actions. His actions always carried heavy consequences. The consequences held a heavy lesson learned. Every time Jon suffered, every painful moment in Jon's life, was for a reason. Jon learned something through each one of his struggles and downfalls in life. He had learned what he would need to know later in life. He would use it on the day that he needed it most. The day he would need to be brave and courageous and stand up against evil. The day he makes a stand against fear! A day like today! Today is that day!

When Dylan now looks at Jon he no longer views him as a bum. Dylan now sees Jon as a man who has become brave enough to overcome his fears. For the first time, Dylan looks up to Jon and can accept him as his Guardian.

52

A blur followed by a flash of light
and a whipping wind sound was the
only thing the Pyramids' watchful
eyes had seen. Seconds later, a dust cloud
followed with the sound of thunder. It was
the Devil himself. He was racing along the
wall of the Holy Land. Bolts of lightning
arched on both sides of the Devil. The Devil
was moving faster than the thunder and the
lightning was having trouble keeping up.
The sand in his wake created a title wave of
sand that buried half the side of the Holy
Land's wall. He was going to cut off Jon and

227

Dylan before they reached the main entrance to the Holy Land. He wanted his book and he was determined to get it.

Jon had been keeping watch on the storm coming from the south. He tapped Dylan on the shoulder and pointed towards the storm. "That's him!" said Jon. "It's the Devil."

Dylan stared at the storm for a moment and then started to look in the book. Dylan found a passage that he could read. None of the words made any sense to him. He chanted the words and a spell of energy shot out of the book and into the air. But, it did not go towards the Devil. The spell went behind them towards the Army of the Damned. The spell formed into a swarm of moths.

The birds of Hell flew into the cloud of moths. The moths ate the condors' wings and bones. The birds were no longer able to maintain flight and pummeled to the ground. Some of the birds landed on the soldiers. Again, the clumsy goons stumbled and fell on the soldiers. But that only slowed down the army. There were many, many more yet to join the ranks.

Jon rested his hand on Dylan's shoulder and said,
"It's alright Dylan. He shall provide us with what we need."
"I hope so, Jon", said Dylan.
Jon replied.
"Have faith, Dylan. Hope is not a definite and is wishful thinking for the future. Faith is what you know. Faith is solid and concrete. It is definite. Have faith!"
Dylan chuckled to himself. The change in Jon was not something Dylan was expecting. Dylan always had to take care of him up to this point. And now, Jon is trying to teach him.
Jon was sincere when he spoke. It was the first time he cared for something other than himself in a while. He even taught himself something while helping Dylan.

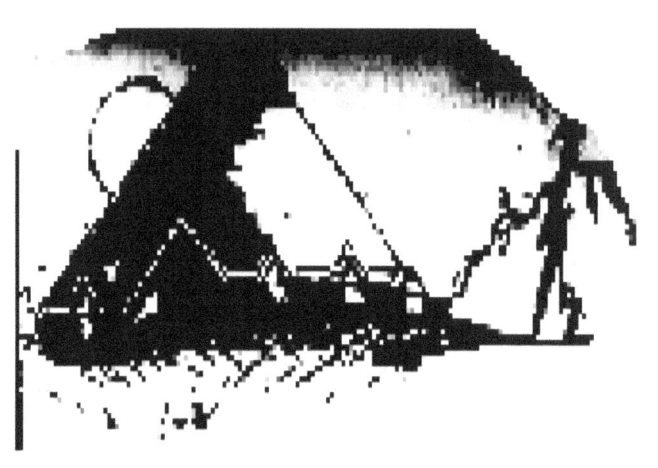

53

AT THE GATES

Jon and Dylan were almost at the front gates when they noticed tiny twisters starting to form in the red sand around the golden path in front of them. At first, Jon and Dylan did not seem too concerned, until they saw what the tiny twisters were doing.

The tiny twisters were sucking up the golden sand and deleted the remaining pathway. All that was left were hills of red desert sand.

Still, Jon and Dylan were only a few yards from the front gate.

Suddenly, a large wall of sand formed in front of Jon and Dylan. They had lost sight of the lightning storm that was traveling down the Holy Land's wall. He had caught up with them. Without any delay, the wall of sand started to twirl and formed into a gigantic twister. All of the tiny twisters joined the big twister, which made it even bigger. Now, the twister was taller than 50 feet. The race was over. The Devil had beaten them to the front gates.

The twister caused Jon to lose control of the dune buggy. They went off to the side of the road and launched off a sand hill. While they were in mid-air, Jon was ejected from the dune buggy. He landed nearby, in the sand. Dylan was trapped inside of the dune buggy while it flipped over several times before it finally rolled to a halt. It landed upside down. The support by the roll bars prevented the dune buggy from collapsing.

A string of lightning bolts traveled up the twister and wrapped around its twirling walls. In the skies above, black and gray clouds were getting sucked into the top of the twister. The roars from the twister shook the ground and echoed across the land.

Jon sat up and watched the twister take form. The twister formed into a gigantic dragon. The dragon stood over one hundred feet tall. The eyes of the beast were the eyes of the Devil.

"So, you thought you could beat me, in my house? On my land! I am god! And soon, I'll be the god of all!" said the Devil. His tong slithered in and out of his mouth like a snake as he spoke. He continued, "You are weak Guardian. You were weak as a human and weaker now".

What did he mean? Jon thought.

Jon looked over at Dylan and saw that he was unconscious. Dylan was hanging halfway out of the dune buggy. The satchel was dangling from Dylan's shoulder and neck. The Devil noticed the satchel and started to run towards Dylan.

Jon lunged forward and tackled the dragon's foot causing him to fall. However, the dragon quickly rose to his feet as if he never even fell. He pointed his finger at Jon. But before the dragon could say anything Jon already had an arrow heading towards the dragon's head. The dragon quickly knocked the arrow down. Then another arrow quickly followed that one. Ten arrows in all were shot at the dragon faster than he had ever seen. The dragon was quick enough to knock down all but two arrows. One arrow stabbed him in the arm and the other arrow that followed went through the dragon's hand as the dragon tried to block it. The dragon finally stood still.

Jon pointed at the dragon and said, "This is the last warning I'm going to give you. Step aside and let us through. All we want is to return home."

This amused the Devil. The Devil began to laugh, but only for a short chuckle. He quickly changed his frown and swung his tail around. His tail smacked Jon across his body which knocked Jon all the way over to the dune buggy. Jon's body slammed into the side of the dune buggy.

234

"Jon, are you alright? Jon!" Dylan said politely as Jon slid down the exterior of the dune bug. He was in obvious pain.

"Oh, hello Dylan" Jon said as he gasped for air. "Nice to see you're awake".

"Everything must be going good?" Dylan asked.

"How do you figure that?" asked Jon.

"Well, I'm not dead yet, I don't think. And you're not dead yet. I don't think. So, that's good. "Right?" Dylan asked rhetorically.

Jon answered anyway,

"The fact that we are in Hell is irrelevant to you? Not to mention I'm getting my ass kicked by a hundred foot dragon."

Dylan cracked a smile.

"That's not funny!" Jon became serious for a moment.

"But you're right. My ass is killing me. I think I broke it. Can you see if there is a crack on it" Jon gave a chuckle and smiled. He then gave Dylan a wink. Jon reached over to Dylan like he was going to help him out of the dune buggy. Instead, Jon grabbed the satchel from around Dylan's neck and started running towards the Holy Land's gates.

"No! Jon, don't do it! No! You won't make it! Jon!" Dylan pleaded for Jon not to go. Jon did not listen. He continued to run without looking back.

Jon reached the front gates. They were closed.

"There must be a key or a door bell?" Jon said to himself. He was surprised he did not see the dragon around. He wasn't to his left. Jon spun around and saw he wasn't behind him. He wasn't to his right. When Jon turned back around to the front the Devil was, standing between him and the gate, face to face. The dragon's face was no more than three inches away from Jon's nose. Jon whispered,

"I'm not afraid of you!"

The Devil had once again changed his form into a scorpion like beast. His legs and tail were the same as a scorpion. His face and body resembled a human demon, only his body was larger and extremely muscular. On the top of his head he grew thick, black horns that gave off a radiant shine. The Devil's eyes were completely black. When

you stared into his eyes long enough you
could see the flames of Hell burning inside
of them. Every shape and form the Devil has
ever taken always struck fear into those who
have had the burden of seeing him.

Dylan suddenly yelled out,
"Jon, look out above you!"
It was too late. The Devil had whipped his
scorpion tail from behind him and stabbed
Jon in the back. His tail pierced through
Jon's back and out his chest. The Devil
lifted Jon up high into the air and
shook him like a rattle. The Devil
roared with victorious laughter. He
then returned Jon so they were face
to face once again.

Jon was spitting up blood. He was
dying. His end was near.
"Give me my book!" the Devil demanded.

Jon did not have the energy to lift his head.
His head laid tilted back. He lifted his
eyeballs to look at the Devil. Jon whispered,
"In the name of the father and of his son"
"What? What did you say?" asked the Devil
bewildered. The Devil was remembering the
time he held his general in the same
situation.

Jon found the energy to lift his head. He looked the Devil right in the eyes and said "And this one's for my spirit!" Jon quickly cut the strap off the bag with a knife that he had hiding in his hand. The satchel fell into Jon's hands and he tossed it towards the Holy Land's wall. It was a strong throw. The thrust of the throw caused Jon to spiral further down the scorpion's tail.

"No!" The Devil screamed as the bag flew through the air towards the wall.

"Not this time!" yelled the Devil.

The Devil had created a ball of power and threw it at the satchel. The ball of power caught the bag in mid air and stopped it from going over the wall. The satchel just hovered in the air under the Devil's control.

"You shall never defy me again!" shouted the Devil.

He became enraged. The Devil lifted Jon way up high and slammed him down to the ground.

"Leave him alone!" a deep and heavy voice spoke from behind the Devil. The Devil turned around to see Dylan.

54

Dylan was standing behind the Devil. He stood slightly turned to his side with one hand tucked in to his jacket. In his background, the Army of the Damned was quickly approaching.

The Devil shouted to Dylan, "Now that I have my book, you are powerless. My army will now destroy you and conquer the heavens. Then, the Earth and the rest of the realms in the universe shall fall. And I shall be their God! I am the New Creator!"

The Devil pointed at Dylan and said, "You, little boy, shall suffer for your friend's ignorance!"

Dylan looked over at Jon's lifeless body. Jon was lying there with his eyes wide open, but lifeless. Dylan had never seen a real dead body before.

Dylan drifted his eyes towards the Army of the Damned. They were closing in on him. They were lifeless beings themselves. So much death surrounded Dylan. Yet, he remained still and calm.

Dylan slowly returned his eyes to the Devil. When he did, Dylan had changed. Something erupted inside of Dylan. His eyes were glowing gold. His flame burned bright to fight his fears. A destiny had been unleashed.

Dylan spoke,
"He is not my friend, he is my Guardian!"
Dylan's voice became really deep and stern. It was just as scary as the Devil's voice.
"And you shall pay for his death."

Dylan took out what he was hiding in his jacket. It was the Devil's book. Jon had tucked it into Dylan's jacket before running to his death with the empty satchel.

55

The book was closed but the cover told a different story. The book was ready to explode with powerful spells. The edges of the book were molting like lava. Dylan's hands ignited in flames. He did not show any pain as he held the book. He lifted the book high in front of him and quickly opened the pages. A powerful force instantly came out of the book and ran though Dylan's body.

"In the name of the Holy Father" Dylan cried out.

Dylan had now turned completely into flames.

 The Devil threw a ball of power at Dylan. At the same time, the Army of the Damned closed in on Dylan and was right above him.

 Dylan released his left hand from the book. A powerful beam of energy traveled up his arm and shot into the sky. The entire sky lit up with three miraculous flashes. Each flash was blinding and had an odd sound at the end of each one.

 The first flash was the worlds of the universe coming to a stop. The sound was treacherous. Everything had come to a halt. The grounds of every planet had stopped. Every realm in the universe had become motionless. Neither a drop of water could trickle nor does a flower sway from the wind. This happened everywhere.

 The next flash had a sound that had a fearfully deeper pitch. It was the sound of time coming to a stop. The dreaded sound

243

echoed all the lands and every being in the universe became motionless. All of the Devil's soldiers slowed to a still. They froze in mid-motion. The swarm of demons attacking Dylan froze right above his head.

Everything had become silent. Even the sound of the wind had been silenced. There was no movement anywhere.

The third flash had a tremendous bang that ended with a cracking echo. It was the sound of a knock on heaven's door.

Dylan had disappeared. He had ascended with the energy beam after the last flash.

The Devil was the only one able to move. The Devil spun himself around and took another form. He had the form of a demon with human details. He observed his army. They all remained motionless in mid-air. The Devil tried to touch one of his soldiers but his hand waved right through him. His hand drifted through all of his soldiers like they were ghosts.

"What is the meaning of this?" demanded the Devil.

56

A bright ball of light appeared from the top of the crack in the Pyramid. The ball of light glided in the air downward toward the Devil. The Devil seemed bewildered at first. The Devil finally realized what the light was. He did not understand why it was here and was angered that it was granted so much power.

It was the spirit of an unborn child. The unborn children are those who had died before birth. They never entered their birth realm.

They are very powerful immortals that are one of God's favorite warriors. God was the father for all the children. They only knew God as their father.

"He grants you this power?" asked the Devil.

Everything remained frozen as the ball of light hovered over top of the Devil.

The ball began to speak to the Devil,

"Once favorite angel of God, again you wish to forsaken him. Again you wish hast into the gates of heaven. Again you bring death where there could be life."
The Devil began to laugh and said,
"You think you know everything? You and your God have forsaken me! You and your God cast me out of the gates of heaven! And it was your God who showed me my power. He showed me my true calling and my forsaken, eternal destiny!" he spoke as if there was another untold story.
  The unborn spirit hovered over Jon and then floated back toward the Devil. The spirit in the light spoke,
"You have killed the father of one of us. The dead spirit, who lies in the sand, he is the father of my own" the spirit paused.
"We forgive you. He will be spared. It is not his time."
He continued,
"Our father, he pleads with you, once again, to cease your attack or you shall suffer the consequences."
  The Devil stood still and stared at the light. Then his face began to frown and he became instantly enraged. The Devil screamed,

"I am a God and the Gates of Heaven belong to God. I am he!"

The Devil swung his tail around and smacked the ball of light. The lighted spirit went flying backwards and crashed into a small pyramid. The spirit quickly bounced back into the air and paused. Then the spirit spoke,

"You have chosen. The punishment has been decided. You shall see the wrath of God!"

The spirit disappeared into the crack of the largest pyramid.

Seconds later, a beam of energy came crashing down from the sky and flowed into the top of the pyramid. The energy going into the pyramid had tremendous power. The power was going to make the pyramid explode.

The other two pyramids opened their tops. The tops twirled and twisted in mechanical motions. Beams of the energy shot out of the tops and into the skies.

The power from the big pyramid was at a constant flow but was relieved by the release of energy from the other two pyramids.

The energy, however, had a purpose and a destination.

"Yes!" the Devil celebrated.

Every piece of sacred land in Hell had lost their sanction and their holy protection was no more. The protection around all of Hell's earths had disappeared and the destructiveness Hell quickly invaded the flourished lands.

The red sand of Hell came crashing on the green flourished lands of the holy. Wave after wave of red sand buried almost all of the holy lands.

At times of Holy War all lands are neutral. This allows both sides to be able to cross over the land's boundaries and not lose any of their abilities.

57

The clouds started to move slowly across
the red skies of Hell. The Army of the
Damned slowly got their
movement back. The wind and
the sand returned to their
normal state and the sounds of
Hell had returned to all of those
ears that are damned to hear it
for eternity.

The army's soldiers all looked at one
another bewildered and confused. This was
something they had not expected. They are
still soldiers and they quickly began to
gather in their ranks. They were fearless.

The gongs of war had begun again. The
sounds of the gongs were so powerful that
all the grounds in Hell had shook. With each
crack of the gong the largest pyramid's

sidewall would crumble. Finally, after a dozen gongs, the entire side of the wall had fallen to the ground. Everything, once again, had become silent.

"What is that?" The demon soldiers asked bewildered. They all looked at their generals, waiting for an answer.

There was a strange sound coming from deep within the pyramid. It was the sound of marching. The Devil and his army looked on with great anticipation. At first glance, they could only make out a blurry white line. It stretched out the entire width of the opening. Another line had appeared behind that one. And so on. The general of the Damned Army held up his shank. On the end of his shank was a clear crystal ball. He looked into the ball and he was able to see over the walls of the Holy Land. The crystal ball gave him the power to view the eyes of the vulture. The vulture was flying in the sky above the city.

The general first saw rows of white lines marching out of the pyramid and through the mazes of the Holy Land's streets.

"What are you?" the general asked himself.

Then, the general focused deeply into the crystal ball. Now he was able to see what was marching towards them.

The white lines were rows and rows of white wings. The wings were curled inward hiding whatever was inside. Like a cocoon to a caterpillar, the wings were guarding whatever was inside.

They continued to march forward. "Prepare for battle!" yelled the demon general.

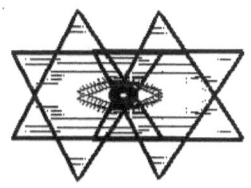

58

The Army of the Damned armed their weapons and formed a line twenty yards in front of the Holy Gates.

The white wings marched through the mazes of the city streets. Row after row they marched up to the edge of the front gates and came to a simultaneous halt. Everything remained still.

The Devil and his army looked on with great anticipation. After several moments, a set of wings had stepped forth. He crossed over from the Holy Land and into Hell, breaking the barrier. The set of wings stood alone in front of the rest of wings. Slowly, its wings uncurled and unveiled what was inside.

It was a baby boy. He was a little baby angel.

The sound of giggling came from the other wings. The rest of the white wings began to open. They too were baby angels. They were an army of baby angels. Their wings and body were outlined with a silver lining and they all stood with their hands folded as they were in prayer. Strangely enough, the baby angels did not have their eyes or their mouths opened. Their faces remained still with an unopened smile. Their eyelids were closed with padded eyelashes.

"Army of Hell, attack!" the Devil commanded.

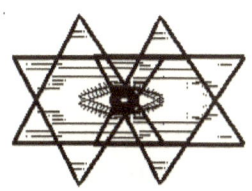

59

The Cherubs are God's fiercest warriors. They are the angels chosen to fight on the front lines against evil.

They are pure. The words of a baby are pure in truth and honesty. Evil does not understand the treasure of truth and honesty. It is painful for them to hear. The sound of innocence is unpleasant to the demons. The Cherub angels use their voice to distract their enemy and take advantage for the kill.

The Devil was aware of how deadly the Cherubs were. He had fought the Cherubs several times before, which mostly ended in disaster for the demon armies. There were battles, however, that the demons had over powered the Cherubs and the Demon army took control over the battle land. A victory

For the demon army will be disastrous for heaven and earth.

The Devil has always commanded his army from afar. Today he is at the first battle. He is leading his army into the gates of glory. The Devil is in his territory, ready to do battle.

"The gates of heaven are opened! Fight! Fight your way into the stairway! Take what's yours!" The Devil commanded his army in an inspirational way.

The Army of the Damned charged to the border of Hell's Earth. The Cherubs were there waiting for them.

As the demons drew closer, the baby angels started to giggle. One after another a Cherub angel began to giggle. Oddly, they had their mouths closed. The sound of their giggling became louder and echoed through the lands.

    The first line of angels stretched out their wings. Their wings connected at each end forming a wall. The rest of the angels prepared the same way. They formed their wings together row after row throughout the city streets and all the way deep into the pyramid.

The wings of the angels were lined with heavenly steel. They were extremely sharp and could never be broken.

The Army of the Damned was about 10 feet away from the front line when the Cherub angels finally opened their eyes. For the first time, the demons looked into the pitch-blackness of the Cherub's eyes. Their eyes were fearful and empty.

The Cherub's laughter became extremely loud when they finally opened their mouths. Their teeth were triangular in shape with very sharp points. Every tooth was thin with a sharp point. The teeth seemed more for an animal then a baby.

The demons leaped towards the angels. The angels squatted down and let out a higher pitched cry. The sound made the demon's ears crack. The demons were greatly distorted. Just as they were about to collide, the Cherubs quickly jumped on top of the demons' shoulders. They sunk their teeth into the demons' necks and feasted until they had eaten through the neck far enough to twist off the demons' heads. Then, without any delay, the Cherub would let out another high pitch cry and leap onto the next demon that was passing by.

All of the Cherubs fought in the same manner. One by one, the Cherubs slaughtered their enemy and would jump onto the next demon without ever touching the ground. They showed no mercy to their prey or to those who got in their way. They gouged the necks of their enemies and let the blood spray sporadically through the air. The blood from their kill would dribble down their face.

When the Cherub took feast, it would shield itself with its wings. They would slice the heads off of anyone or anything that tried to interrupt their feast.

The bigger demons were harder to kill. The Cherubs mainly attacked them by a swarm. It took a team effort in order to defeat the bigger demons.

The Cherub's sound had little effect on the bigger demons. The Cherubs would attack their legs to try and trip them to the ground. The Cherubs would fly by the larger goons' legs and slice them with their wings. Once a demon, of any size, had fallen to the ground the Cherubs would swarm the fallen demon and eat its flesh down to the bone.

The Cherubs killed in a gory manner. Once each head of the demon was ripped from its neck, their bloody corpses were left to spill out onto the grounds of Hell. The demon's blood would absorb into the sand and their bodies turned into red or black ash.

One of the demon soldiers used his ball and chain to hit one of the Cherubs. The Cherub was smashed to the ground. The baby Cherub started to cry. Several other baby Cherubs were feasting nearby. They heard the cry of their fallen brethren. The baby Cherubs immediately stopped eating and lifted their heads. Blood was dripping down all of their faces. They all let out another kind of cry. One of their brothers had fallen and needed help.

The baby angels came to assist the fallen angel. When they arrived the demon was over top of the baby Cherub. His back was turned, so nobody could see what he was doing. The demon slowly turned around. He held the lifeless body of the baby angel in his hands. The demon had just snapped the baby's neck and sank his teeth into him. The demon looked up and smiled at the one Cherub standing in front of him.

"Huh?" The demon noticed another Cherub had joined from behind him. Another Cherub had joined from the far side and another from the right. The demon was no longer smiling. He turned around to run away but when he turned around there were six other Cherubs closing in on him.

The Cherubs started crying. The cry shattered the demon's ears and all the demons' ears that were nearby were distorted too. The demon staggered a couple of steps backward. Two of the Cherubs had positioned themselves underneath the demon's legs and caused him to trip over them. The demon fell on his back and was facing up. The Cherubs circled around him. The demon pleaded for the Cherubs not to hurt him. The Cherubs did not listen.

The Cherubs had surrounded the demon. They spread their wings so there was no escape. The Cherubs slowly closed in on him. They opened their mouths, it was time

260

to feast. Their wings blocked the view of them feasting on the demon.

When the Cherubs were finished with their feast they flew away. All that remained of the demon were bones, the ball, the chain and a nose ring which one of the Cherubs had burped up. The ring spun in the air and landed onto the bone of the demon minion.

61

The Devil had magically appeared at a command post set behind his army's frontlines. All commanders of war have given orders from behind their front lines. This is where a commander could think of his battle plans and give the commands to carry them out.

Whenever one of the Devil's battle plans did not work, he would throw one of his minions far into the battlefield, killing whatever it landed on.

The Devil led his campaigns of war fearlessly, with no mercy, no remorse, and no regrets. At many times he was careless and gave no remorse for the lives he sent to

Hell's Earth copyright © 2015 by Pete Trolene
All Rights Reserved

their end. He did not have a care for their demise.

He ordered his troops to bring up the catapults and multi-arrowed crossbows. They worked well for the Devil. They kept the Cherubs out of the skies.

The Devil sent word across Hell for all demons to come and fight in the battle. There are generations of families living in Hell. Many had their ancestors make a deal with the Devil, which damned the generations of their families to Hell. They are the innocent ones. They may have done nothing wrong while living on Earth but still have to suffer the consequences in their afterlife for their ancestor's actions.

All of Hell's damned creatures had to join ranks and fight against the holy or face the agony torture from the Devil. The pain from his torture was unimaginable. There were some who did die right away from the torture. They were the lucky ones.

More and more demons and damned creatures of Hell approached from afar. Some of them flew in the air. Others traveled on the ground. Every type of life form that ever existed, like the dinosaurs, began to travel towards the battlefield. The Devil's message had been sent through the land and will continue until the end of Hell's time.

Every life has consequences. Every life of every species at every time must fulfill their consequences before they can move on. Every sentence into Hell is unique. Some sinners had ways to repent. Others did not have any alternative but to remain here as slaves. There are also those who choose to be in the Devil's service. They have the blackest soul. They are granted special abilities, special strengths of whatever the Devil sees fit.

Those who are deemed useless to the Devil are cast out into the red desert sands of Hell. They have no food and no water and they cannot die. They are in constant hunger and extreme thirst. These beings were usually the first to fight in battle or die for whatever the Devil saw fit. They were used to spring any traps set for them or they were used as bait for their own traps. Their human lives had long been forgotten and nobody cared for their soul. They are truly the forgotten souls.

The demons and the damned became stronger as they approached the Holy Land. They grew in size and strength. They all had red glowing eyes. Some grew horns. All of the forgotten were possessed and eventually turned into a full battle demon. This power of transformation was given to them by the Devil.

The Devil and his army will never give up. They will never run out of soldiers. The wars of Heaven and Hell do not last for days or months or years. They last for centuries!

This is another reason the Devil fell back behind his ranks. Like the piece in a chess game, your king is the most protected.

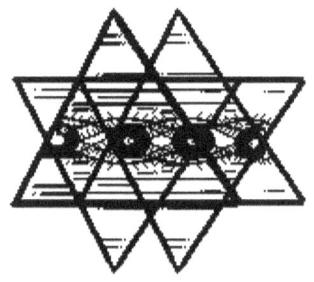

62

It appeared that Dylan had turned into the energy from the book and ascended with the rest of the power that went into the sky. Even though he was lifted into the sky, Dylan was falling through the vortex without any control.

Dylan heard voices calling his name as he fell. They wanted him to join them.

"Come and join us! Try to find us!" the voices had sung out to Dylan. They chanted hints of how to ride the wave of power through the vortex. They told him there is a way to control your journey. The ones who are in an understanding of life, death and the universe are the ones who can control the ride the best. Some people call them time travelers.

Several vibrant colors flashed by Dylan as he traveled through the vortex. He was falling and spinning out of control at a high speed. He became frightened. He started to hyperventilate and then everything went black.

63

Narration

It has been told Dylan ended his journey at the end of his universe. This was the point where there was no time. There was no day or night. There was no right from wrong. This is the point before the blackness became light.

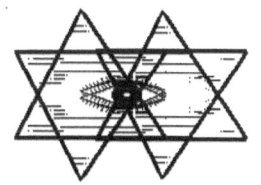

This is where Dylan learned the ways of the universe. He learned the truth of our existence. He learned the secrets of mankind and of all the life in the universe. It has been told this is where God taught Dylan the reasoning between right and wrong and the necessity of having death and life. This is when Dylan found out that mankind was not far from being able to understand and accept the true facts about life, death and the universe.

Dylan had become a chosen one by God. One of many in the network of living beings that have important destines. He was chosen by God to know the truth and to share that truth with the rest of his world.

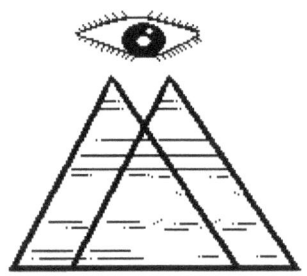

64

Dylan opened his eyes. All he saw darkness. It was total darkness. He could not see the clothes he was wearing or his hand in front of his face. He was not cold nor was he hot. He did not feel any wind  or air. He could not hear anything, only his thoughts. The strangest thing was there was no floor. There was no ground. Yet, he was not falling or being thrown upwards. He was just, there.

A little white light floated down into Dylan's hands. Dylan cupped the little light and took a closer look at the light. To Dylan's amazement the light was a tiny ball. Inside the ball spun stars and planets. The more Dylan stared into the ball the more he understood the universe.

The light started communicating with Dylan. Dylan remained motionless as he listened to the light.

"Yes. I understand." Dylan replied to the light.

Dylan let go of the light and it slowly levitated into the air. Dylan began to float away from the tiny ball of light.

A ray of light shot out of the tiny ball. Dylan looked on with great excitement. The ray of light burst into hundreds of particles. The particles circled around Dylan. They started to grow in size. All of the particles were spinning and twirling around Dylan. Soon, the particles turned into boulders. The boulders turned into mountains and the mountains grew into entire countries. The countries grew and turned into continents. The continents turned into planets. The planets turned into solar systems. This beam of light was the beginning of a galaxy.

Everything circled around Dylan. It was an extreme run of a galaxies life span. The life cycle of each planet would play through in front of his eyes in fast motion. Every life form would grow and evolve on each planet. Their entire life and death would run through his head. A whole lifetime of experiences from each planet and all the life forms that lived on that planet would run through Dylan's mind.

   The life forms living on a planet would start to die and eventually become extinct. This upset Dylan. But Dylan saw that every time there was darkness there was a spark that followed. Life would try again. Each time there were life forms that evolved. Most of them have been able to escape extinction. But they all changed. They all had to evolve with their planet. Life began to grow. Life would travel from planet to planet. The more Dylan watched the more civilizations appeared. While all of this was given to Dylan he knew there was still something missing. All the knowledge of the universe needed something clse.

   The sun circled closely around Dylan. The sun grew bigger then Dylan and was growing bigger quickly.

Dylan started to spin. Around and around he twirled and twisted. The sun was now moving faster than before. There was so much motion that eventually everything became a blur.

Dylan let out a scream.

Suddenly, all of the planets and stars started to get smaller. Everything started to slow down. The planets were reversing in nature. Instead of the universe expanding it started to get smaller and enclosed around Dylan. The entire universe shrunk down into a tiny ball of light that floated softly down into Dylan's hands. Dylan gently cupped his hands. Everything went dark.

65

The Devil's army was on the verge of breaking through the Holy Land's walls. They had the Cherubs backed up against the city's gates. This was not a surprise to the Devil though. He was well aware that the Cherubs don't like to go far from their nest. 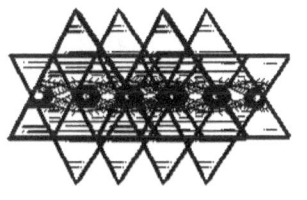 The farther away from the Holy Land, the weaker they were. The Cherubs like to fight on their own turf. That is where they were most powerful.

A General had ordered a Boned Bird to swoop down and kidnap a Cherub in a sack. As the bird flew away, the kidnapped Cherub put a small slice into the sack. He pushed his head through the hole and let out a cry for help.

Several nearby Cherubs heard the cry and tried to save the baby. When the Cherubs finally caught up with the bird, they were really far away from the front gates. The Cherubs were drawn away from their nest.

The Demon General took notice to the chase and ordered his soldiers to assist the Boned Birds. By the time the demons came to help the demon it was too late. The Cherubs had ripped the head and winds off of the Boned Bird.

The General reported everything that had happened to the Devil.

66

The Devil had ordered a cease-fire of the catapults. The Damned Army's front line had started to fall back. 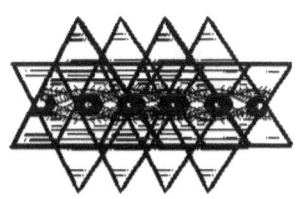 The damned soldiers started to scatter apart as they ran away into the desert. This caused many Cherubs to take chase. The chase did not last long. The Devil had altered the sky's horizon so the Boned Birds could not be seen. The Birds would swarm out of the hidden horizon and grab a Cherub with their claws, but not to kill. The captured baby Cherubs were held loosely so they would be able to cry for help.

The Cherubs would bite at the Boned Birds'
ears, legs, and neck. Others were placed in a
wooden cage.

Nearby Cherubs would come to help their
brethren. They would try everything to save
their brethren.

The Boned birds waited until they had five
or six Cherubs on them and then the Boned
Birds would swoop down to low ground.
The Devil then raised his arms and sand
demons emerged from the ground. They
swallowed every bit of the Boned Birds as
well as the Cherubs that were attached to it.

Once the Cherub's front lines were spread
out, the Devil once again lifted his arms.
This time, catapults emerged out of the
sands. They bombarded the Holy Land's
front lines with boulders of fire. He killed
the Cherubs as well as the Boned Birds. He
killed everything. Whatever did not hit in
the air, hit on the ground. Some fire-
boulders hit the walls of the Holy Land,
causing the walls to catch ablaze. This
enlightened the Devil. The burning wall of
the Holy Land was a pleasure for the Devil
to see.

The Cherubs were taking a beating from the strategies of the Devil. His next move proved to be most devastating to the Holy Cherubs.

The Devil created a humungous boulder of fire and threw it into the Holy Land's front gates. When the boulder hit the gates there was an explosion, which caused a blinding cloud of smoke. When the smoke had lifted, the gates of Heaven had been blasted to pieces and left smoldering on the ground. All of the Boned Birds, Cherubs and warriors that were near the gates during the blast were incinerated. Ashes and charred Cherubs covered the grounds. This is a small price to pay for the Devil. Now, the gates of heaven were wide open.

"Now charge!" the Devil commanded.

Hidden under the sands were several desert demons. The Devil had used his power to alter the land as he did with the sky and the Boned Birds. The demons popped up out of the sand and began to charge with their weapons drawn. Demon

279

after demon charged in through the gates of the city. They ran through every street and alleyway.

   The streets of the city were not like any other city. These city streets formed a maze. No matter which street the demons ran down, the maze had always ended at the same place, at the entrance to the biggest pyramid.

   Just inside the pyramid is the stairway to Heaven.

67

Once the demons had beaten the Cherubs back to the opening of the biggest pyramid, someone was there to meet them. The person stood at the top of the stairs that led into the pyramid. He wore a dark cloak with its hood covering their face. The only thing showing was the Devil's book hanging from their shoulder on a chain.

The book's cover had turned into heavenly silver. The strap was a heavenly silver rope chain. Two worlds were outlined on the cover of the book. One was for Earth. It had a blue and gold outline. The other was for Hell. Hell was outlined with red and gold.

Having the book change into this form could only mean one thing. The book had been blessed with divine power. Unlimited powers of the universe had been granted to the one chosen to be the books keeper. The keeper was Dylan.

Dylan stood tall in front of all those demons. He had seemed a lot taller and older. But none of that mattered. Dylan had more knowledge then any man who ever lived. With knowledge came power. The demons feared the power of knowledge.

The demons stood and stared in bewilderment at Dylan as he raised his hands in the air and the book magically levitated in front of him. Dylan had lifted his head and his eyes shined a blinding light. Dylan was ready to battle.

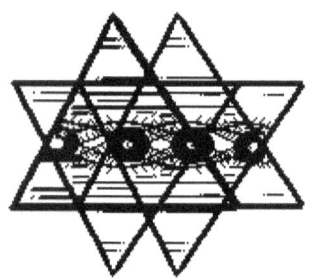

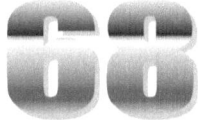

68

Past the fiery debris of the front gates and
over a sand dune laid Jon's
lifeless body. He laid facing
up and his arms stretched
above his head. His slightly
opened eyes read death.
Jon's only motion was his
clothes blowing in the wind. Not a breath or
a blink. He had been dead now for some
time.

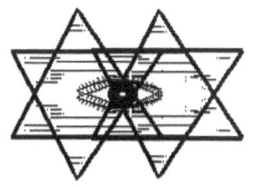

The spirit of the unborn child (the same
spirit who had appeared to the Devil earlier)
floated out of heaven's broken gates and
hovered over Jon's lifeless body. The light
looked over Jon's arms. Jon had marks and
holes on his arm. They were wounds of a
different kind of battle. These scars were

283

from his addiction that took control of his life on earth.

"Oh, my father, please learn to forgive her." the light whispered to Jon.

The unborn spirit circled around Jon. Then it entered Jon's body through Jon's mouth. Jon's eyes brightly lit up. His body jolted and started to shake profusely. He quickly sat up and then quickly lay back down. Jon's body laid flat and he started to levitate. Odd circles of light circled around his body. They were like the rings of distant planets. They made a peaceful noise. Jon's body started to spin and the circles kept their tempo.

Jon's wounds had started to heal. Everything healed except for the holes on his arm. The holes turned black and sticky, like tar. They bubbled on his arm and then finally froze solid. It looked like onyx stone.

"May you never forget, Jon"

A loud cracking sound came from Jon's back and Jon let out a horrifying scream! Jon's eyes opened wide. He was alive!

69

Dylan had battled Hell's Army all through the city's streets. He slowly walked down each path eliminating the demons. With  magical powers that flamed through his hands, Dylan was able to disintegrate many demons at one time. Sometimes, he was able to kill fifteen to twenty (15-20) demons with one blast.

His powers had tremendously grown. God's light and the powers of the holy book flowed through Dylan. And God's light shined bright.

The demons were not able to get around Dylan. The streets forced the demons to "bottle-neck" and fight Dylan head on. If they sent too many soldiers at one time they would get smashed together between the walls and Dylan would send a mighty blast, killing them all.

Dylan walked atop the ashes of the dead demons. Not even the bones of the damned were able to withstand the force Dylan had unleashed upon them.

Most of the demons had started to retreat. Others would throw a spear in fear and desperation and then run for their life.

Dylan was able to create a magical force field that would block any projectiles thrown at him.

Dylan had found his calling. He now knew his responsibility. Dylan had now become a Guardian. Dylan's mission is to keep the book out of evil's hands.

70

The Devil began to enter the front gates with another platoon from his army. Thus far the Devil was pleased to see that his strategies had worked so well against the Cherubs. It has been centuries since his soldiers last infiltrated

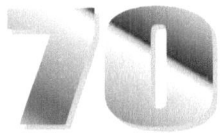

the Holy Land gates. And soon, they shall be knocking on heaven's door. Only without his book, the Devil cannot open the door.

All of his army had orders to find the boy and the book. They were to bring back his book at any cost.

The Devil called one of his minions over to give him an update. The minion replied with absolute fear. He stuttered his every word. "Well, My Lord, We found the boy…"

Hell's Earth copyright © 2015 by Pete Trolene
All Rights Reserved

"Excellent! The Book?" the Devil asked.
"We found the book but…"
"Bring them here. Now!" demanded the Devil.
 "I am afraid to report…" the minion demon began to say but was silenced by the Devil's gesture. The Devil was overlooking the near-by horizon. He could see his soldiers flying through the air and over the Holy Land's walls. The rest of the soldiers were retreating. A soldier ran up to the general and yelled, "It's the boy, my lord."

   The Devil instantly grew tremendously large and crushed the messenger with his hand as he rose to his feet. He had taken the form of a beastly demon. His stare was directed toward the entrance of the gateway. "Where are you?" the Devil whispered to himself.

The anticipation grew to see if it really was the boy who was destroying his army. The Devil's face built up in anger. He started to huff and puff. Again, he began to grow in size. He grew five times his already monstrous size. He towered over the wall of the Holy Land and was now as tall as the smaller pyramids. His arms bulged out so

288

big that nobody could see around him. His head had become hideous, as each horn grew thicker than any giant tree. His bottom half had taken the shape of a gigantic demon bull.

The Devil started brazing his leg as he prepared to charge. When the Devil had looked at the entrance once again, Dylan had already been standing there.

71

Dylan's hooded garment was covering his head as he stood at the entrance to the Pyramid. The book was levitating behind him with a silver chain attached from the book to his side.

The Devil started charging towards Dylan. He barreled forward and stepped on his own soldiers, squashing them onto his hooves. He ran faster and faster and quickly built up a lot of speed and momentum. His army charged behind him.

Dylan stood with his arms crossed at the entrance of the Holy Land. He waited patiently for the Devil's assault.

The Cherubs lined themselves up on each side of Dylan. They all had closed their eyes and mouths. Their wings were laid back and their hands were in prayer formation. They seemed peaceful standing there waiting with Dylan.

Silence fell upon Dylan's ears. All of the soldiers, warriors, Cherubs and animals of war seemed to move slowly to Dylan. Dylan could see everything around him at one time. His peripheral visions allowed him to see his complete surroundings. His vision was so enhanced he was even able to see moments into the future. Dylan's mind was in a state of total control. Even the motions of the Devil seemed slower.

The Devil was about 20 feet away when the Cherubs quickly flapped opened their wings. Their eyes and mouths had opened wide and they screeched out a heavenly cry. The cry was a pleasant sound to the heavenly beings. But to the demons it was torture. The demons held their heads in a panic as the sounds echoed through their head.

The heads of the demons had exploded. They could not handle the cry of the Cherubs. The sounds from the Cherubs, however, had no effect on the Devil.

The Devil had crouched down as he prepared to lung forward and ram Dylan. The Devil's face crunched in and smoke came out of his nose. His eyes became bright red then turned into a fiery yellow.

With the size of the Devil being so big, Dylan had no chance to go around him. Dylan had no chance at going over him. He had no escape. He was going to have to take the Devil on head to head.

The Devil took a mighty leap at Dylan, "KABLAAM!" It was a sound mightier than thunder.

A small, white object had soared down from the sky and struck the Devil on the head. It knocked the Devil to the ground with his face hitting the ground first. He hit the ground so hard that he had made a title wave of sand that rippled for miles.

A dust cloud had covered the entire area, blinding the entire area. When the dust had finally settled, the Devil laid face down on the ground with a white, feathery object on top of his head.

Dylan had stood his ground. He did not move, not even once.

The large set of white wings covered the Devil's head and hid the body of the winged creature.

There were gigantic chain links lying on the ground around them. They had a magical glow.

Neither the Devil nor the white winged creature had moved for many moments. The wings were not of the Cherub or of the Demons. The wings were something Dylan had never seen and had no knowledge. He was in wonder, "Why would the Lord of Goodness give me all the knowledge of the universe but have not have given me the knowledge of these wings?"

Dylan realized at this moment that there was still knowledge he did not know about in the universe. Dylan then thought, "How silly of me to think I would be able to carry all the knowledge in the universe."

That much knowledge would be too much information for anyone to bear alone. Dylan believes the Lord will give him what he needs and when he needs it. It is up to him to have the faith in that belief and the trust that his faith will not give him more than he can handle.

Dylan finally lifted his head and removed his hood. His face had the frown of bewilderment. It was awkward for everyone at that moment.

Finally, the wings started to slowly unravel open. The barer of the wings had been revealed. It was Jon.

Jon had the wings and the markings of a Guardian Angel. Jon had grown physically and spiritually. He prospered into a trusted servant of the Lord. He had a meaning. He had a destiny.

Jon had a good start on fulfilling his destiny. He had stopped the Devil from ramming Dylan. He fulfilled his first task as a Guardian.

Jon slowly rose to his feet. His chest expanded out as he took a deep breath. His body had never been so fit. He stood on top of the Devil with the arrogance of a champion. Brave, courageous, honorable, strong and spiritual are some of the words that describe this moment in Jon's life. The noblest warriors

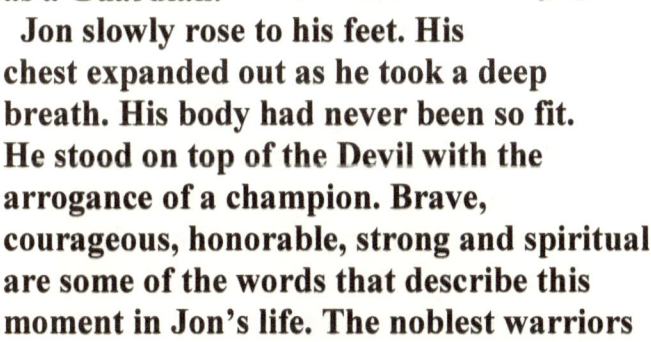

honor all of these virtues and Jon was short on none of them. This is what Jon had always wished for his life to represent. Jon had lost his ambitions in life when he lost his wife and baby. But now he is reminded of his purpose in life, to be a servant of all that is good.

Jon grabbed each tip of the Devil's horns and yanked them together behind the Devil's head. Jon wrapped the Devil's horns together with a thick heavenly chain. Jon was about to seal the chains with a lock when the Devil opened his eyes and instantly began to shake his head. The Devil rapidly shook his head up and down and then in circles. Jon was thrown far in to the air but was able to regain control with his wings.

The Devil quickly rose to his feet. The lock and chain loosened and fell beneath the beast. The Devil was not happy. Smoke rose out of his nostrils and his eyes were gleaming with an angry red color. The Devil held his arms out to his sides. His arms started to spin. They spun so fast that his arms turned into twisters. The twisters began to suck up all the demon soldiers that were near. As the demons entered into the

Hell's Earth copyright © 2015 by Pete Trolene
All Rights Reserved

Devil's vacuums, the Devil grew twice his already humungous size. He now towered over all the small pyramids. Only the one tallest pyramid was the only thing bigger than him.

"You are no match for me," said the Devil.

"A Guardian you may be," said the Devil. He raised his arms in front of his body and a blaze of fire shot off his arms and through the air towards Jon. The shot nipped Jon's wing. The wing singed like paper in a fire.

"A Guardian you will die!" said the Devil.

Jon immediately flapped his wing to stop the burning. At first it made the singe worse and his wing became a blaze. The flame finally went out after Jon rolled his wing inward and smothered the fire. This was Jon's warning from the Devil. The Devil's message was simple, he can and will kill with no mercy and no regret.

The Devil fired once again upon Jon. This time the fire was stopped by a magical water shield that Dylan had thrown from the far side.

"Ah, the thief in training," said the Devil about Dylan.

"What do you think you're doing boy? Is it all right to take something because it's for your side? Anywhere else, in the universe, they call it stealing and it is considered a crime. Or even worse it is a sin."

The Devil talked to Dylan in a calm voice. He began to pace back and forth. The land shook with every step he took. The Devil's size was tremendous compared to Jon and Dylan. The Devil stood taller than most giants. This did not seem to bother Jon or Dylan. The power of courage had helped them overcome their fears. With courage and faith any man can handle any obstacle before them.

Jon circled around the Devil in the air. Not once did Jon turn his back on him. Jon was dealing with the prince of darkness and deception. Dishonesty was in the Devil's nature. Jon was without any doubt that the Devil will smite him at the first opportunity.

Oddly, the Devil's attention was more focused on Dylan.

"You have my book. Boy. Is it not mine? The book has been taken from me. Should you not return the book to its owner? Is that not what is in your nature? Do you not give back from the taken?" The Devil spoke as if he were the victim. His words were soft and calm and very convincing.

"It is not yours if you stole it first," Dylan replied.

"Ha! Ha!" the Devil began to laugh.

"Who do you think wrote the book?" said the Devil.

"Do you think your God wrote it himself?"

The Devil stopped pacing. His voice became angry.

"No! He called upon me to write it for him. He used my hands, my arms, my fingers. I even wrote it in seven different languages for father. I wrote it! Therefore the book is mine!"

The Devil once again had to regain control of his temper. And he did, so very well. He almost instantly became casual.

"You have a lot of talents, boy. You could be a great influence to the people on your planet. Would you not like to have that privilege?" asked the Devil.

"Would you like to have the power to save your people, to tell them the truth?"

"Return the book to me. Then I will return you home to your world. You tell your people the truth. You tell them what prevailed here. Let all of those around you know the truth about deception and the true meaning of self-sacrifice. Tell all those who hear your word to tell all those that they know. And those people shall tell all they know. Let your message spread like a wild fire. Let the knowledge in the universe burn through their minds. Then they will need guidance. Every person who hears your words will come to you for your leadership. It is for you to rule. They will ask for your direction. And who better to give it to them then you? They will need your guidance. They are very simple minded. They will need discipline. Give it to them," the Devil's voice was very compelling.

"Those who do not ask for your divine wisdom or those who do not take lesson from your knowledge will be the ones who destroy the world. Anarchy will run wild in the streets.

You are the key to their salvation. You will teach them justice. You shall hunt down all of those who oppose you. All those who oppose you are those you wish for life to perish. They must be brought to justice. Have them do everything your way, the right way. They will perish if they do not follow your rules. Only you can show them the way. Your way, your way is the only way. Let it be done."

The Devil's words were sincere. The power of his voice crept into Dylan's head. The voice kept repeating its self over and over. With each thought, the temptation for evil became stronger.

"Do you not want to help your people? They cannot survive without your knowledge. You do want to save your people, don't you Dylan?" These were the words repeating in Dylan's head over and over again.

Dylan knew he had to change his thoughts. And quickly, before it was too late. He kept thinking about what the Devil had said and he could not think of anything else. It kept echoing through his mind. Soon he will be under the control of the Devil.

Dylan knew his time was just about up. But what was Dylan going to do? What could he do? How could he ask for help?

Jon saw the look in Dylan's eyes as Dylan was trying to fight off the images in his head. It was a look that Jon knew all too well. It was a feeling of hopelessness and emptiness. He came across the same feeling every time the craving for a drug crept into his head. It was a battle within your own mind. And nobody was going to help. Nobody accept someone who knows what is going on. Only the addict truly understands this feeling of hopelessness and despair. It was easier just to give in to the craving for the addict. And the times the addict decided to fight, the addiction won the battle eventually.

Jon remembers these thoughts of hopelessness.

Jon remembers that feeling that there was no other way to go. He remembers looking at the end of his tunnel and seeing darkness. Jon remembers how that powerful feeling took his life to the bitter end.

Jon was not going to let that happen to Dylan.

Jon thought,

"He's only a kid, for God sake. If that power was a battle for me then it must be ten times worse for the kid. I must help him."

Jon felt responsible for Dylan. Jon felt the power of caring.

Jon angled himself downwards toward Dylan.

"Not on my shift," Jon said as he arched his wings behind his back and flapped them downward. The thrust gave him enough power to soar towards Dylan very quickly. But the Devil was quicker. He stuck out his arm and smacked Jon to the ground.

"You two alone do not have enough power to beat me." said the Devil.

"And soon it will be just one of you."

Jon had hit the ground so hard that he created a crater where he crashed. The impact was devastating. Jon laid there motionless. The Devil lifted his gigantic hoof to stomp on Jon and finish him off forever.

Dylan noticed a giant crossbow across the way from him. It was already loaded with an arrow and aiming towards the Devil. Dylan ran over to the crossbow and grabbed the lever with both of his hands.

"This one's for Meredith," said Dylan. Dylan pulled the lever backwards as hard as he could. The lever released a latch which in turn shot off the crossbow and released the giant arrow into the sky. The arrow hit the Devil in the back of his standing leg. The Devil, once again, came crashing down to the ground. The wave of sand threw Jon's body up into the air. Jon started to awake while he was in the air. He shook his head awake and opened his eyes. He immediately regained control. He saw the Devil lying on his back. Jon reacted without any delay. He flew down to the heavenly chains and used all his strength to throw them over the Devil's neck. The chains lapped over the Devil's neck and locked at their links. The chains magically tightened. Jon held the bitter end of the chain to the ground.

A few Cherubs helped put the chains around the Devil's feet at the same time. Their chains magically tighten also. The Cherubs also held down the loose ends of the chain to the ground.

"Hopefully this shall hold the beast!" said Jon.

Then, all went silent. Dylan had appeared atop of the Devil's chest. The atmosphere became very grim. The motions of the sky had paused and the wind had vanished.

Even Jon seemed surprised to see Dylan with the Devil.

"Dylan? What are you doing?" Jon asked.

Dylan did not answer. Dylan closed his eyes put his head down to his chest and covered his head with his hood.

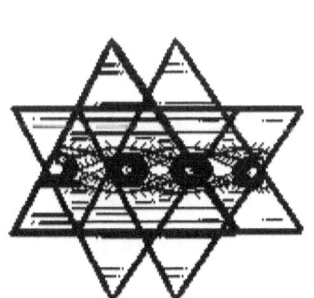

305

73

The Devil began to awaken.

"What is this?" demanded the Devil. He tried to sit up but the chains around his neck magically tightened with his every move. Jon and the Cherubs held the bitter ends in place on the ground.

"I am ridding you, for now," said Dylan in a calm and almost sarcastically kind of way.

"I know who and what you are," said Dylan. Dylan began to walk around on the Devil's chest.

The Devil responded,

"You cannot get rid of me! You do not have such power! My master has all power here. I am merely a marble in my master's hand. There are many rulers like me. He will call upon all the powers of the universe, if I need

306

so, they will come down from the fiery skies above and kill you all in my honor!"

The Devil slowed down and became relaxed. It was strange to see the Devil relax on the hope of a power greater than himself. "Look all around you. Can you feel him? Can you taste him? You breathe him in. He is everywhere. Even on your little planet. Wherever your God is not, he is. And one day, he will be always and always will he be! "

Dylan uncovered his hands. Twirling above Dylan's hands was the little white feather he was entrusted with earlier. "Like all the powers in the universe?" Dylan replied.

"No. It can't be, Father?" The Devil cried out. And then the Devil got his answer.

The red sky behind them began to part. The sky had cracked. Then the dark red sky thunderously spoke to the Devil. The sky was evil. The sky is the power the Devil worships. This evil force is the opposite of everything that is good.

The sound echoed of pure evil, but the Devil understood everything the sky was saying.

"I have failed? No. Father, please, not yet!" The Devil cried out for his existence.

The red skies fell silent. Then something strange happened. A very bright light ascended from the crack. Very slowly the light drifted towards them. As the light came into focus it took the shape of a person. It was a spirit but not like the other spirit they saw before. This spirit had human characteristics. One of which reminded Dylan of someone he knew back at home.

The sky had sealed closed and the evil atmosphere had disappeared.

The lighted person floated down and landed next to Dylan on top of the Devil's chest. The lighted person looked over towards Dylan and gave him a gesture as if it was time for Dylan to begin. Dylan nodded his head as if he understood. Dylan removed his hands from underneath the feather. The feather drifted above Dylan's head in a circular motion. The feather was twirling around in a playful manner. The feather fell to the Devils chest and continued to twirl. Dylan and the lighted person held out their arms to surround the feather.

The Devil was starting to get extremely upset. It was getting difficult for Jon and the Cherubs to hold down the bitter ends of the chains.

Jon did well as an acting commander. He commanded the Cherubs to get a boulder and drop it on the Devil's head. The Cherubs did so and it knocked out the Devil for a couple of moments. He also came up with different strategies to hold down the Devil. Jon had earned the trust of a leader.

Even though the feather seemed playful, Dylan was aware of the power it carried. The feather started to twirl faster. Soon, the feather caught up to its own tail and soon passed its tail again and again many times over.

The lighted person and Dylan held each other's arms to keep control of the feather. The feather had now turned into a tiny twister. Dylan and the light held the twister in between their arms and bodies. The tiny twister, however, was rapidly growing and becoming harder to control. It was still a thin funnel but moving very fast.

309

The lighted feather grew extremely fast. The oddest thing about this twister was that it did not suck up any objects. No sand, no dust, no rocks, not soldiers or their weapons. The twister was not even picking up the wind. It seemed to be a cyclone with no power.

The lighted person released one of their hands and waved it towards the deserts of Hell. As they waved their hands, a wave of power had surged from the side of the cyclone and traveled in every direction through all the lands. The wave had surged through everything and everyone but only the remaining soldiers of the damned were affected, leaving the Cherubs unharmed.

The damned soldiers were instantly incinerated by the wave of power. They turned into red glittery sand and floated in the air. These sands were the only thing the

310

twister began to collect. All of the red sand drifted towards the cyclone.

The red sands blew past Jon and the others with screams of horror and hatred.

The whirling sounds of the cyclone were also fearfully thunderous and became more fearful as more soldiers of the damned joined the cause.

When all the red sand from the damned soldiers was collected, the lighted person and Dylan returned their arms to reconnect with each other.

Dylan had centered his head. He took a deep breath and closed his eyes. Then Dylan removed his other arm from the lighted person and waved it towards the Holy Land.

Once again a wave of energy was released from the side of the cyclone. The wave of energy was a different color. The power of the wave was different as well. This wave had a different purpose. This time the wave was meant for the Cherubs. Their work was done here and it is time for them to return home.

The wave of energy had sung a song to the Cherubs to put them asleep before washing over them with a wave of death.

The Cherubs turned into glittery white and gold sand. They blew away with the wind, just as the demons, but in a joyful manner as they ascended into the cyclone. When they blew past with the wind there were sounds of joyful singing. A sound of victory trumpeted in the wind and the sound of giggling babies pranced in the air. They were going home to see their father. The Cherubs were happy.

"Good-bye, Dylan! Good-bye Guardians!" said the voices of the Cherubs.

After all the Cherubs were collected Dylan returned his hand to the lighted person. For a moment all was silent. It was sad to see the baby angels go. They had fought such a strong-hard battle.

Suddenly, the twister became out of control.

75

All whom remained were Dylan, Jon, the lighted person and the Devil. The cyclone had been spinning extremely strong on top of the Devil's chest. The cyclone grew upward and became wider towards the top. As the cyclone franticly spun around, stars, planets, suns, and moons were popping in and out. The cyclone had all the powers of the universe and they were spinning out of control.

The Devil awoke and shook franticly, despite how tight the chains had become. He had become desperate as he saw he had no more army and his times end was near. "What? No? What are you doing? No!" yelled the Devil as he shook his body with tremendous strength. He was still unable to go anywhere despite his efforts.

"It takes so long! Damn you boy! I shall have your blood line! I will return! I will boy! I will have my revenge!"

Dylan and the lighted person let go of each other at the same time. The Devil tried to break free but only managed to launch Dylan far into the desert dunes when he jerked forward.

Jon wanted to escape but was too late. Jon and the lighted person quickly secured themselves to the Devil as the cyclone's wall passed over top of them. Jon, the lighted person and the Devil all became trapped inside the cyclone's funnel.

Dylan was the only one on the outside of the cyclone. The cyclone was growing wider and bigger very quickly and was heading towards Dylan.

Jon had pinned the Devil's horns back down with his wings. Jon could not move anywhere without releasing the Devil's horns.

Jon looked at the Devil's feet. The Devil was starting to erode. The Devil's hooves and ankles turned into black sparkly sand and smoke and disappeared into the cyclone. The Devil could not withstand the power of the cyclone much longer. His enormous size and his powers made it harder for the cyclone to demolish the Devil. But the cyclone grew much stronger then the Devil. The Devil became over powered.

"Guardian, you have not seen the last of me!" yelled the Devil.

Jon replied,

"Just for today is good for me for now."

Jon held down the Devil's horns as the lighted person stood on top of the Devil's chest. Jon looked up at the lighted person with concern. The walls of the cyclone had them trapped inside with the Devil. There was no escape and the walls were closing in on them.

Jon had loosened the chain around the Devil's neck. On the Devil's last attempt to get up, Jon used the thrust from the Devil to throw himself through the cyclone's wall. Just as Jon let go of the Devil's horns the lighted person immediately rewrapped the horns and pinned them back down to the ground.

First the cyclone finished off the Devil. He did not make a sound. He crossed his arms and closed his eyes as the cyclone sucked up his remains.

The person of light, the mystery person of who was so much help had turned into a thin, straight bolt of energy and shot herself into the sky.

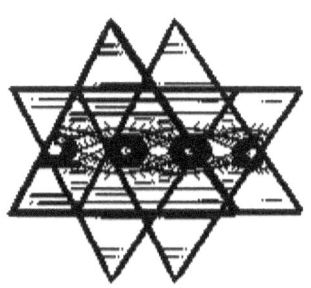

76

Outside the funnel the cyclone's wall reached high into the sky. Its width grew wider than anyone could see. The cyclone was very powerful and wildly out of control.

The Pyramids stood halfway eroded as there golden walls turned into sand and blew away into the cyclone.

Dylan ran away as fast as he could. The cyclone grew on him fast. The sand was being sucked up from underneath his feet. Dylan was not going to make it.

The cyclone was about to swallow Dylan when Jon swooped down from the sky and picked him up right before the cyclone was about to swallow him.

Jon flew them away from the cyclone. Jon and Dylan looked for a safe place to land. There was nowhere to go. The cyclone had swallowed everything. And as Jon and Dylan looked back, the cyclone had become so big they could not see around it or over it. The cyclone had no end.

Jon flew as fast as he could to get away from the cyclone. No matter how hard he tried to fly away it was not enough. First, the remaining clouds flew past them and then the rest of the sands had followed. Finally, the skies and all the remaining colors vanished into the cyclone. Everything was now nothing.

"The Devil is merely a puppet for evil"

77

Everything was in total darkness. There was only one sound. The pounding beat of a heart. That is all Dylan could hear. He stood on top of a white marble pillar. It is the same pillar Jon had in his dream. It was an endless pillar of time.

Dylan looked down and saw no end to the darkness. Dylan was scared. The heart that was beating seemed funny and different. "Is that my heart beating?" Dylan wondered to himself. A white feather had floated down from above and landed in Dylan's hand. Dylan closed his hand tightly and promised to never abuse his power.

"I must never use this on earth, the consequences could be disastrous," said Dylan. "If humans knew what they are actually capable of doing they would all kill themselves."

He reopened his hand.

"My knowledge is my power. No human may acquire this knowledge until they have evolved enough to handle such abilities."

The feather turned to ash and crumbled in his hand. The ash drifted away into the darkness.

The sound of Dylan's heart began to increase. Deep in the background of darkness an object appeared.

"Is that something?" thought Dylan. "Should I yell for them? What if they don't know I'm here? I could be out here forever? Can I fly? Do I have the power to fly?"

All of these thoughts had raced through Dylan's mind. He even had a thought about Jon and his old life. He wondered if it was as difficult to overcome an addiction as it was to climb up this pillar.

Dylan waited quietly on the ledge of the small pillar. He could see the object was getting bigger.

"It must be getting closer," thought Dylan. "It must be coming for me. Why else would it be out here?"

Suddenly Dylan didn't feel so good. The thought that something bad might be coming for him crept into his mind. His body began to shiver.

"The heart that is beating, is it mine or his?" Dylan thought.

"What if it were a beast? The heart beating is not mine. It is the beasts!"

Dylan closed his eyes and formed his hands in prayer.

"Dylan! Can you hear me?" Dylan heard a voice. It was not God's voice but a voice he was familiar.

"Jon!" exclaimed Dylan.

Dylan opened his eyes and put a big smile on his face.

"I'm over here!"

Jon glided up to Dylan with his wings extended and fully repaired.

"How are you? I bet you're glad to see me? Again," Jon said with a chuckle. "Hold on, I'll get you out of here."

With one last pass Jon scooped up Dylan and swung him onto his back.

They flew for a short distance. Jon told Dylan about his experiences with the lighted person and that she was safe with God.

"She?" asked Dylan.

"Yep, the light was a lady." Jon replied with sarcasm.

A strange object appeared in the distance. It shined a red light. They flew towards the light. The light then turned blue. And then white. As they became closer the light it turned red then yellow.

Dylan could now see that the light was a door. It was a door like the one he used when he first stepped into Hell's Earth.

"This is your stop, buddy," said Jon.

"My stop, are you not coming Jon?" asked Dylan.

Jon had set Dylan down on the step in front of the doorway.

"Oh, I'm coming with you all right. I'll just be watching you from a different point of view," Jon gave Dylan a smile and a wink of security.

   Dylan took one last look at Jon and said, "You have done good Jon Welsh, and good shall come onto those who do well."
Dylan stepped through the doorway and entered into the other side.

78

There was complete darkness. Dylan felt scared. The door slammed shut after he fully entered into darkness. The door magically spun around in circles and had shrunk down several sizes until it finally ended as an object the size of a book. Dylan caught the object in his hands and saw that it was indeed a book. The book was the book Dylan had originally found back at the old church.

Dylan squeezed the book tight and took a step into the darkness. Dylan began to fall. He fell and spun out of control. But Dylan had faith. He stayed calm and held the book tight. He closed his eyes and kept them shut. A few seconds later Dylan could feel that he had stopped falling. He still kept his eyes closed. He took a couple of deep breaths. There was a scent he was familiar with. He smelled the aroma of a church. Dylan's body immediately began to relax. He opened his eyes. When he finally looked up he saw he was back at the old church.

The room was warm. There were dim lights throughout the back of the church. "You better pick that up before someone else finds it!"

A voice said from behind Dylan. Dylan noticed that his book was on the floor. "People can be like demons around here. They'll steal things right out from under you!" A man walked over from the far side of the room.

Dylan took notice to the man's black shirt with a white collar. He was a man of the clergy. The man stepped into the light. He was overweight and wore glasses. Dylan took another look. It was Jon. He was in a priest uniform. It did not look like Jon. "Jon?" Dylan asked.

"Hello Dylan. For you, you are on time. For me, well, let's just say I've been waiting awhile for you. Welcome home." Jon walked over to Dylan and greeted him with comfort. "You have returned a few moments in time before your friends get here. Just return home and I'll scare off your friends when they get here. It is as if it never happened." said Jon.

"The book should remain on this holy ground. I will watch over it. If and when the book needs you, you will be notified."

Dylan had bent down to pick up the book. As he did the wind had blown open to a page with a sketch drawing. It showed a picture of a boy who was knelt down by a book with a shadow of a man standing over top of him. The picture in the book was of them at that exact moment in time. The story was theirs. Dylan realized the story was about destiny. He felt as if the journey was not yet over. The book had closed and that destiny had been fulfilled.

THE END

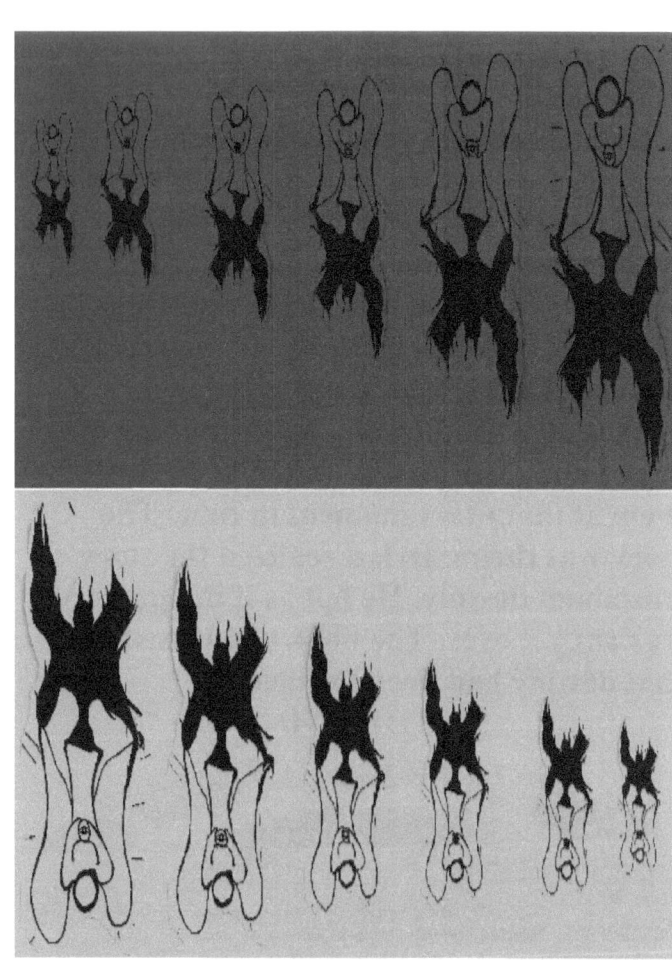

EPILOGUE

The Devil stared into his visionary pool which was filled with souls of the time that had past. He flipped through the pages of a book. In the black water of his magical pool was the vision of Jon dressed as the Priest at an old church. The Devil smiled and said, "I know what you want, Jon Welsh. I have what you want!"

The Devil started to laugh as he ran his fingers through a woman's hair. The woman was bruised and dirty. She was weeping and would cry if she only had the eyes for her tears to cry. Her eyes and mouth were sown closed.

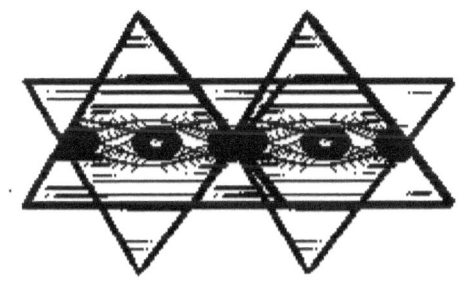

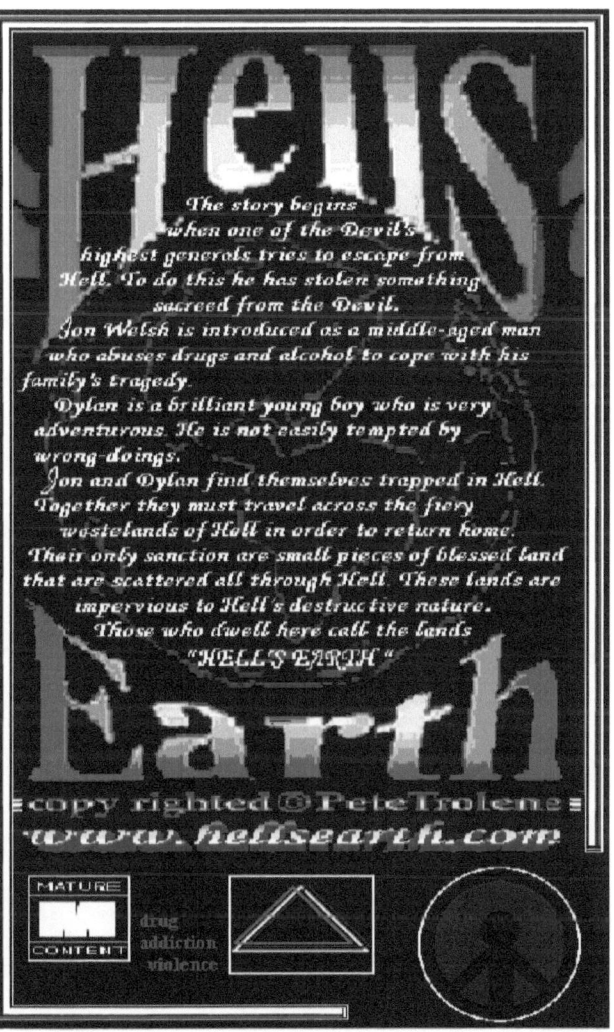